THE CHILD SHE NEVER SPOKE OF

THE BOWERS HILL SAGA

NELL HARTE

Copyright © 2025 by Nell Harte

All rights reserved.

No part of this book may be reproduced in any form or by any electronic or mechanical means, including information storage and retrieval systems, without written permission from the author, except for the use of brief quotations in a book review.

DISCLAIMER

This story is a work of fiction, any resemblance to people is purely coincidence. All places, names, events, businesses, etc. are used in a fictional manner. All characters are from the imagination of the author.

WOULD YOU LIKE A FREE BOOK?

Join my Newsletter
 Receive A Subscriber Only Book
 CLICK HERE FOR
 THE BEGGAR URCHINS

CHAPTER 1

Hail drummed against the sash windows, a fierce wind whipping down the streets of London, creeping in through every gap and crack it could find. The whistle of it provided an eerie chorus to the sky's relentless percussion. But inside the dining room of the Calder household—lovely, comfortable apartments on the nicer side of Saint Pancras—the roaring fireplace and the hearty feast on the table kept the cold and the inclement weather at bay.

"You must be careful," Caroline Calder warned, beaming from ear to ear, "or you shall spoil me rotten, and I'll start getting notions."

Her father, Adam, began to carve the magnificent leg of lamb that had been roasting for hours, filling the entire apartments with mouthwatering aromas. "If ever there was a day to be spoiled, it's one's birthday. You are only four-and-ten once."

"But if you truly feel that way," Caroline's mother, Heather, interjected with a playful smile, "then perhaps I shouldn't let you have a slice of the cake that I made. It's your favourite, too."

"I'll have her slice!" Caroline's younger sister, Esther, declared, raising her hand. At ten years old, she was rather more mischievous than Caroline, who had been trying very hard to appear more mature, now that she was at the vast age of four-and-ten.

Caroline chuckled, so happy she thought her heart might burst. "I think I'll have some cake, and just promise not to be spoiled. After all, I wouldn't want you to have gone to so much effort, Mama, only to not get a taste."

"An excellent decision," Adam said, putting a thick slice of the delicious lamb onto a plate and passing it to Caroline.

She took it gratefully and set to work, piling the rest of the plate with crispy roasted potatoes, cooked in dripping; thinly cut carrots coated in honey, sweet parsnips that had become deliciously chewy at the narrowest end, and a helping of pickled red cabbage.

She waited politely until everyone else had a full plate in front of them, before they all clasped their hands, closed their eyes, and professed their gratitude for the meal they were blessed to have. On such a bitterly cold day, with a storm that showed no sign of abating, the Calder family never let themselves forget how lucky they were.

A decade ago, though Caroline could not remember it well, they had existed under entirely different circumstances, inhabiting a two-room terraced house near Seven Dials. Still lucky, by anyone's standards in London, but not quite as fortunate as they were now, with rooms aplenty, all the food they could desire, and an education that the two girls would not, otherwise, have had.

"Thank you for this wonderful meal," Caroline said to

her mother, who preferred to cook, rather than employ a cook to do so for them.

Her mother smiled. "It is my pleasure, dearest Caro." She hesitated, glancing at Adam, who gave a subtle nod in reply. "But there is something else that we should be grateful for, whilst we're celebrating such a happy day."

"What is that?" Esther asked, already tucking into her dinner.

Adam reached out and took his wife's hand, his eyes alight with love for her. "You are to have a brother or sister."

Caroline, who had just brought a piece of succulent lamb to her lips, lowered her fork so quickly that it clanged against the side of the plate. "We are?" She stared at her mother in disbelief. "Do you mean it? Are you truly with-child?"

"I am," Heather replied with a shy smile, her eyes watering.

Esther swallowed her mouthful quickly. "When will they be here? When can we meet them?"

"In around five or six months," Heather said, her cheeks flushing with pinkened joy. "The physician told us last week, but we thought you might want to hear the news on your birthday, dear Caro."

Caroline clapped her hands together, so overcome with emotion that tears began to well in *her* eyes too. She was a firm believer in miracles, but she had never witnessed one in her own life. Yet, there it was—a miracle she had hoped for as much as her parents, for she had often overheard them whispering of their wish to have another child, and of their disappointment when month after month, year after year, went by without one. There had been losses too, quickly covered up, never mentioned, but grieved over in private between the husband and wife who adored one another like newlyweds, even now.

"I think this shall be the best birthday ever!" Caroline crowed, grabbing her glass of cloudy lemonade and lifting it in celebration. "To our new brother or sister!"

Esther grabbed her glass too, not wanting to be left out, and clinked it against Caroline's. Their mother and father joined in with their glasses of red wine—a recent gift from a contented client of Adam's that had been opened for the occasion.

"To your new brother or sister," Heather said, as Adam brought her hand to his lips and kissed it tenderly.

They all repeated the sentiment, sipped from their glasses, and began to eat the delicious meal that they had been blessed with. It had already been a joyous occasion, but the mood was even brighter, the atmosphere a little giddier, the dining room even warmer as they shared the feast together, knowing that there would be a fifth member of the family soon enough. Another chair filled at the timeworn table, to increase their happiness and good fortune.

"You will have to paint a new portrait of us," Caroline said, closing her eyes in delight as she savoured the taste of the roast potatoes and the lamb, so tender it was practically melting in her mouth.

Her father laughed. "I had enough difficulty with the last one, between the two of you refusing to sit still, and me being unable to get my own face right. I still think I look as if I'm squinting, or that I've smelled something horrible."

"Nonsense, Papa," Caroline protested. "You look exactly the way you look."

He feigned horror. "Goodness, I must remember never to show my face in public again then, if that's true."

"Your eyes are a *little* squinty," Esther conceded. "In the portrait, I mean. They're not squinty in real life."

Heather hid her mouth behind her hand as she laughed. "Except when you come back from working all night long in your studio. *Then,* your eyes are a little squinted, my darling. You always look like you have spent too long staring at the sun, and I *always* tell you that you shall ruin your eyes."

"I can't help it, darling," Adam protested, grinning. "Once inspiration seizes me, I can't leave my studio until the feeling passes. When I ignore it, I start drinking tea and reading books, and I get nothing at all done."

Heather raised an amused eyebrow. "Ah, so *that* is what really goes on at your studio. I knew you couldn't always be working yourself to the bone. I mean, sometimes, you come back from your studio only *half* covered in paint."

"I fear I shall always be a messy painter," Adam said with a dramatic sigh. "I don't know how these other portraitists do it without getting a speck of paint on them. Part of me wonders if they are not really doing the painting at all, and they give it to their apprentices to do."

Caroline smiled at the exchange between her mother and father. For as long as she could remember, they had always been playful with each other, mocking and teasing and laughing. She had assumed that was what all parents were like with each other, until she had been invited to have tea at her friends' residences and had realised that her own parents were the exception. Most of her friends' parents did not even seem to like each other at all.

"Will you be considering apprentices, now that Mama is with-child?" Caroline asked.

Adam pulled a face. "I simply can't do it. I don't have it in me to teach others how to paint. I barely know how *I* manage." He offered a comforting smile to his wife. "But I *shall* be working less, so that I can spend more time with you all. Fewer lengthy nights, certainly, even if the inspiration tickles."

Heather leaned into him, smiling joyfully as Adam pressed a kiss to her sandy-coloured hair and put his arm around her, holding her close; both of them lost in their own bubble of love for a moment.

At just turned four-and-ten, Caroline knew it was far too early for her to be thinking about her own marriage and what sort of gentleman she might like for a husband, but she knew one thing for certain: when the time came for her to start contemplating marriage, *that* was exactly what she wanted. A marriage of love, displayed without shame or embarrassment, where she was as much her husband's dearest friend as she was his wife.

* * *

STUFFED full of rich food and a slice of sugary, buttery cake apiece, it would have been easy for the Calder family to retire to the parlour to enjoy the warmth of the fireplace and to spend the night in sleepy peace, digesting their exemplary dinner. But that was not their way, particularly on birthdays and Christmas and when they had something else to celebrate.

Holding their stomachs, groaning of how full they were, they put on their cloaks and coats, wrapped themselves up in scarves and hats and gloves, and headed out of the middle-floor apartments and down the stairs to the main entrance together.

Outside, the hail had thankfully decided to stop, replaced with a drizzling rain that would undoubtedly be frozen into a treacherous ice slick by morning. It had already been the most miserable January Caroline could remember, in terms of the weather, though she would not complain of it. Not when they would assuredly pass countless families and lost souls who had nothing, not even a roof over their heads, on their way to Sadler's Wells Theatre.

"Remember to stay close to each other," Heather warned. "Girls, hold hands."

Dutifully, Caroline grasped Esther's hand in hers, though the younger girl protested.

"If you fall, Caro, don't you dare drag me down with you."

Caroline laughed. "But if *you* fall, will you expect me to keep hold of you?"

"Of course," Esther replied with a smirk.

They set off into the bitter night to walk the half an hour it took to reach Sadler's Wells where, in the tangled and strange gardens, there was an old well. Its namesake, whispered to be holy, the waters medicinal to soul and body and mind alike.

Caroline did not know when it had begun, but it was their family tradition on birthdays to go to the well, make a wish upon the trickling waters, and to take a sip, praying their wish would come true. Although none of Caroline's wishes had ever come true, she had never doubted the magic of that well, and she decided that, on this night, she was going to make the very best wish she could. After all, she had proof now—the well and the made wishes *did* have power. Her mother's happy news was all the evidence she needed.

"Your hand is clammy," Esther murmured, stifling a giggle.

"How can you tell? Have you put another hole in your gloves?" Caroline replied, rolling her eyes.

Esther grinned. "I can just feel it."

They walked along the wet pavements, heads bowed to the drizzle, following their mother and father through the labyrinth of London's streets. Despite knowing that the city could be dangerous in places, Caroline never felt a jot of fear when her father was with her. He might have been an artist, but he was strong and protective and would never let any harm come to a single one of his family.

"Are you still there?" Caroline called back.

"Who?" her father replied, playing the game.

Caroline smiled. "Our mother and father *should* be right behind us."

"I'm afraid I don't know who your mother and father are," Adam said in an apologetic tone. "You must be lost. I should take you both along to the river where the rest of the little ducks live."

Esther groaned loudly. "Papa, we're not babies anymore!"

"I must protest!" Adam insisted, as he rushed forward to scoop his arms around his daughters. Chuckling, he kissed them both on the head as he declared, "You'll always be my babies, and you'll always be my little ducks."

Esther peered up at him, a smile cracking her face. "Very well."

He hugged them both before falling back to walk with his wife once more, the four of them warmed by their affection for one another, no matter how cold the city might be.

At length, the Calder family arrived at the Sadler's Wells Theatre: a striking building with whitewashed walls and dark timbers forming crosses on the exterior, echoing the style of the Tudors. It was beautiful to behold, but the theatre itself did not have the most favourable reputation: a nest of vice and unsavoury characters who had no interest in the revues and performances taking place on the stage, deeming it more of a music hall where they could do as they pleased.

Still, the night was early, and the ruffians and degenerates would not appear at the venue for many hours, after they had drained the public houses and inns dry of their ale and liquor.

"I hope you have your wish ready, Caro," Adam said, leading them through a gate to the side of the theatre, where steps led into the strange, somewhat wild gardens.

They had been pleasure gardens once, designed around the well as a sort of spa where the wealthy could come along and sample the restorative waters whilst enjoying themselves in beautiful surroundings. But the idea of such healing waters had fallen out of favour, and the Sadler's Well had been all but forgotten.

Adam guided them through the overgrown paths, holding aside brambles and briars and clawing branches for everyone to pass through, until they came to the stone façade—worn and weathered and lichen-covered—where the well trickled its mystical waters into a hollowed-out curve.

"Go on, sweet girl," Heather encouraged, nudging Caroline forward.

Caroline took a breath, nerves suddenly prickling through her veins. Ordinarily, this was just a merry tradition that she enjoyed, but never expected much from. However, it held a different weight that night; she worried that if she did not make the right wish, or make it hard enough, it would not come true. And, now she *knew* that they could come true, it was almost overwhelming to try and decide upon just one thing.

She stepped toward the stone bowl that caught the water and put her hands beneath the narrow channel where the water trickled out. The droplets soon formed a small pool in her palm, enough to sip.

I wish... I wish... I wish that—

Her secret thoughts were interrupted by a voice calling out, startling the wish right out of her mind.

CHAPTER 2

"Is that you, Calder? It *is* you!"

A gentleman in a fine three-piece suit, swamped by a dark greatcoat, entered the small courtyard where the well could be found. There was a boy, of similar age to Caroline, at the man's side, though he did not look at all happy to be there. The boy's grey eyes narrowed at the sight of Caroline's cupped hands beneath the well water and raised a fierce glare up to meet *her* bewildered eyes.

What did I do to deserve a scowl like that? It was not as if it was water that belonged to anyone, nor did anyone have to seek special permission to come into the gardens. Yet, the boy continued to glower at her as if she was doing something wrong.

"Quentin," Adam said, his tone surprised. "What an unexpected pleasure."

The gentleman reached for Adam's hand, shaking it vigorously. "I was just up there when I saw you. I couldn't believe my eyes. How long has it been?"

"A couple of years, at least," Adam replied.

Caroline vaguely remembered the man, Quentin Rawle,

and remembered thinking him strange before. Not too much had changed, though her father seemed relatively pleased to see his old acquaintance. If Caroline was not mistaken, the two men had lived together when her father first came to London as a young man, pursuing his artistic ambitions.

Quentin glanced at Heather. "Still the luckiest man in England, I see." He laughed, gesturing to Esther and Caroline in turn. "Goodness, your daughters have grown! I swear they were no taller than my knee when I last saw them."

"Do not remind me," Adam groaned. "They grow up far too fast. Indeed, it is my eldest's birthday today, and I was just telling her that I should prefer it if they would always be my babies. And who is this?" He nodded toward the scowling boy. "This must be your sister's boy, is it not?"

Quentin patted the boy on the shoulder. "Yes, my nephew. His mother is unwell, so I am taking care of him for a while." He gave the boy's shoulder a subtle squeeze. "Greet my friends, Luke."

"Pleasure to meet you," the boy, presumably named Luke, grumbled.

Nephew? Caroline observed Luke discreetly, noting a few similarities between the boy and Quentin. They had the same grey eyes, wolf-like somehow, and the same strong chin and jaw—though Luke had not quite grown into his yet. There was something in the eyebrows too, though that was where the similarity ended. Where Quentin's hair was a non-descript shade of brown, Luke had hair the colour of freshly cut hay; his complexion ruddy and freckled where Quentin's was pale and untouched by the sun.

"Forgive him," Quentin said with a tight smile. "He is

still getting accustomed to being away from his mother. She spoiled him, I fear."

Luke lowered his gaze, his posture rigid, his hands curled into fists, but he said nothing in retort.

"Seeing as it is a celebratory evening," Quentin continued, gesturing back at the theatre, "why don't you join me and my nephew at the evening's performance? I have something of an investment in the theatre, you see, and it would be my honour to have you all sit in my private box with me."

"Can we?" Esther chirped, tugging on her father's arm.

Caroline, meanwhile, glanced at her father uneasily. She need not have worried; the small frown etched across his brow reflected her own feelings on the matter.

"Another time, perhaps," Adam said politely. "It's cold and I'm eager to get my family back home."

Quentin waved a dismissive hand. "Another time, of course. No matter." His smile attempted to reach his eyes and failed. "It is so very good to see you, Adam. And you, Heather. You must come to dinner soon, both of you. Your dear daughters too. I have recently moved to Mayfair, and I have not used the dining room once!"

"Mayfair?" Adam nodded appreciatively. "You must be doing well for yourself."

"It would be impolite to say," Quentin replied with a wink.

It looked like he was about to say something else, when a different voice cut through the muted serenity of the well gardens.

"I told you it was him!" a woman cried excitedly, pulling a gentleman towards the gathering of people. "You *are* Adam Calder, are you not?"

Adam smiled shyly. "I am, Madame."

"My mother just commissioned a portrait from you, at my recommendation. I do not suppose you remember us, do you?" the woman asked, blushing furiously whilst the gentleman at her side—her husband, perhaps—offered an apologetic look.

Adam frowned for a moment, then smiled. "I *do* remember you. Mr. and Mrs. Harcourt, if I am not mistaken?"

"Darling, did you hear that?" the woman screeched. "He remembers us!"

Adam chuckled. "I rarely forget a client, Mrs. Harcourt."

"I was just telling my husband that we must have another portrait done, for I have recently learned that I am with-child," Mrs. Harcourt said, divulging more than would have usually been considered appropriate.

But Caroline could not help but smile at the scene, charmed by the knowledge that her father and his work were so famous. Mrs. Harcourt was not the first client to cheer Adam's work with such open enthusiasm—nor, Caroline hoped, would she be the last. No one painted the way her father did. No one captured the essence of people the way he did, though it was a great pity that neither she nor Esther had inherited their father's talent.

Perhaps, our brother or sister will be as gifted as him...

"What happy news!" Adam said, taking hold of his wife's hand and kissing it tenderly. "We have been similarly blessed. Indeed, nothing makes you prouder or happier than one's children and family—wouldn't you agree?"

Mrs. Harcourt nodded effusively. "I could not have said it better myself. And I can think of no one better to capture our new happiness than you, Mr. Calder."

"If you send word to my studio, we can begin a discussion," Adam said.

As Mrs. Harcourt continued to wax poetic about the particular skills of Caroline's father, Caroline herself was watching the expression of Quentin Rawle. There was a peculiar flicker of something unpleasant in his eyes, his gaze briefly fixed on Caroline's mother, his lip twitching, all the mirth gone from his expression.

A moment later, that strangeness had gone, replaced with a beaming grin.

"Why did you not tell me about your joyful news, Calder?" Quentin asked loudly, clapping Adam on the shoulder. "Now, I *really* must insist on you all coming to dinner so that we can celebrate properly."

Adam laughed. "We shall arrange something but, as you can see, I am about to be rather busy."

"As ever, my good man," Quentin said, the cheer in his voice somehow too bright to Caroline's ears. "But truly, I shall not take 'no' for an answer."

The group of adults continued to talk as Caroline and Esther hung back, the latter stifling a yawn and rubbing her full stomach. The boy, Luke, cast his steely gaze towards the stone bowl where water still trickled, curiosity creasing the corners of his eyes.

Following his gaze, Caroline realised that she had not yet made her wish, and it appeared that everyone else had forgotten the purpose of their visit to those strange gardens.

Turning back to the shallow bowl that caught the water, the curve of it coated in a glistening layer of some kind of algae, Caroline put her hands beneath the rudimentary spout, collecting just enough for a sip.

I wish... Goodness, what do I wish for?

"What are you doing?" The boy had appeared beside her, his voice as sharp as his expression.

She ignored him, struggling to concentrate in the wake of his proximity.

"She's making a wish," Esther said blithely, apparently oblivious to Luke's sour attitude.

The boy scoffed. "Aren't you too old for silly games?"

Caroline continued to ignore him, closing her eyes as she allowed more water to gather in her cupped hands. *I wish... for the baby to be healthy and happy. I wish for the baby to change our lives for the—*

"Caro?" her mother's voice interrupted her secret request. "Come on, darling. We ought to be leaving; it's getting late."

"Coming, Mama," Caroline replied, shooting a glare at the boy who still stood smirking at her as if he thought her very stupid indeed. He could think what he liked; *she* knew that there was power in that well, and there was nothing silly about it at all.

Not wanting her wish to go to waste, even though it was unfinished, she quickly sipped the water from her hands. It tasted of earth, faintly metallic, and as it slipped down her throat, she prayed that it would come true, certain that whatever forces granted such wishes had known how she was going to end her plea.

CHAPTER 3

The windowpanes throbbed as mighty winds bombarded the city, the sky bleak and swollen with encroaching storm clouds. On the streets outside the Calder apartments, unfortunate citizens were bent double against the blowing gales, coats and cloaks flapping backwards like broken wings, little spirals of dead leaves and city detritus spinning upwards, while more was whipped along the pavements.

"This is all my fault," Esther lamented from the window seat where she sipped tea like the elegant lady she would, undoubtedly, one day become.

Caroline quirked an eyebrow at her younger sister. "How so?"

"I wished to not have to go to school today."

Caroline chuckled. "You didn't drink the water. I hardly think the heavens would conjure a storm just to prevent us from having to go to school."

"How else would you explain it?" Esther offered her sister a pointed look, apparently still convinced that she was the creator of the inclement weather.

The two girls attended the North London Collegiate School, situated in nearby Camden Town. An experiment, as some called it, into the equal education of girls by the pioneer, Frances Buss. Many looked down upon it, mocked it, thought it distasteful, thought it obscene, but Adam and Heather Calder could not have been more encouraging of their daughters and the pursuit of their education.

"Who is to say that the school will be closed?" Caroline pointed out, fastening a ribbon in her hair.

Esther shrugged. "I have a feeling, and I'm rarely wrong."

"Are you ladies ready?" their father asked, rushing into the parlour, searching for something. "We're leaving imminently, and if you're not out the door with me, then—"

"You'll leave us behind," the two girls chorused in unison, well-acquainted with their father's morning warning.

Adam paused to laugh, shaking his head before resuming his search. He crouched to peer underneath the two armchairs and the settee, before digging around beneath the cushions of the latter. A moment later, he produced a rectangular leather pouch, raising it high in the air as he cried triumphantly, "A-ha! You can't hide from me!"

"You ought to put a string on that, and tie one end to your wrist," Caroline teased, for her father was always losing his pouch of long, thin charcoals.

He wafted a dismissive hand. "The panic is good for me. Gets my heart racing every time." He pocketed the charcoals and straightened the front of his waistcoat. "Now, shall we?"

"I'm telling you, the school will be closed," Esther remarked, slipping down off the window seat.

"If so, we can all come right back and take care of your mother," Adam said, ushering his daughters out of the parlour and along the airy, bright hallway to the front door.

He popped his head around one of the doors that branched off from the main hallway. "Darling?"

"Yes, my love?" came Heather's raspy voice. She had been up most of the night, unwell due to the life growing inside her.

Caroline, who had always been a light sleeper, had heard every disturbance, wondering if it was a sign that her wish would not come true, or if such sickness was to be expected.

"Would you like me to fetch you something for luncheon? I thought I might visit the apothecary too," Adam said, worry in his voice.

"Don't fret, darling," Heather replied. "Go about your day as usual. I don't need anything special. I just need some rest and I'll be quite well."

Adam hesitated. "I'll bring you some soup."

"Very well," Heather said with a soft, husky laugh. "If that will make *you* feel better, then soup would be a pleasant thing."

Adam chuckled in the back of his throat. "You know me too well, darling. I love you."

"I love you," Heather replied, raising her voice as she shouted, "And I love you two—my sweet girls. Be careful of the wind and rain and learn everything you possibly can. Soak it all up, my darlings, and remember how lucky you are!"

Caroline expelled a relieved breath, her suspicions confirmed that what her mother was experiencing was normal. "I love you, Mama! Rest well!"

"I love you more, Mama!" Esther chimed in, nudging Caroline in the ribs.

"No fighting!" Heather called out, her tone laced with amusement. "Go on, off with you! You are disturbing my sleep."

Grinning, Adam retreated from his wife's door and scooped his arms around his daughters, forcibly ushering them out of the apartments and into the ferocity of the gathering storm.

* * *

BY THE TIME they arrived at the North London Collegiate School, it became obvious that Esther's prediction had come true. One of the schoolmistresses stood by the gates, apologising to the girls as they arrived, informing them that Frances herself had deemed it too dangerous for everyone to be in the building in such awful weather.

"What did I tell you?" Esther whispered gleefully, as the trio retreated from the school.

Adam stood in the violent winds for a moment, the tail of his greatcoat snapping like a boat sail, his hands on his hips as he visibly contemplated what to do with his daughters.

"You'll have to come to the studio," he said, a short while later. "Yes, today you're going to continue your education in how to draw."

He nodded to himself and turned into the ferocious wind, eyes watering against each gust as he set off, his two daughters in tow.

It was not often that Caroline and Esther were allowed to visit their father's studio in Covent Garden, and Caroline could not hide her excitement as she hurried along after him, eager to see his latest work. He was a surprisingly private man when it came to his paintings and portraits, and despite being famous in society for his masterpieces, Caroline could count on one hand the times she had actually seen his artistic creations.

"We'll stay at my studio until noon, then we'll fetch soup and medicine for your mother," Adam said as they walked, his voice barely audible above the howling winds. "I want one half-decent drawing out of each of you by then."

Caroline and Esther nodded in agreement, grimacing as dust and dirt flew up and struck them in the face, a few motes determined to get into their eyes. Nevertheless, they were in high spirits as they walked the forty-or-so minutes from Camden Town to Covent Garden: a route that their father usually took alone after he had escorted them to school. It was a novelty, and no mistake. Caroline did not believe that her sister was responsible for conjuring the storm, for she had not gone through the proper process of making a wish, but she was certainly grateful for the fierce winds. Even as the icy rain began to pour in fat, angry droplets, soaking all three to the bone with half the journey still to go, she refused to complain.

The trio resembled drowned rats as they ran the last stretch across the piazza of Covent Garden to the studio—a high-ceilinged attic above a bakery and a lawyer's office, the space shared with a poet who never seemed to be there. A partitioning wall constructed of several triptych screens that Adam had painted and created himself separated the two halves of the attic, to allow for some privacy on the rare occasion that the poet decided to make use of his half.

"Don't touch anything," Adam warned mildly, as he shed his sodden layers, hanging them on one of the rafters to dry.

The two girls did the same, positioning themselves on the worn chaise-longue tucked away at the back of the studio. There, they received paper and charcoal, before Adam set about arranging a scene for them to draw: an apple, an old ceramic jug with a crack down one side, and a spoon.

"Remember light and shade," he told them, before wandering off to the other side of the space, where a huge canvas stood in front of a high stool and an equally tall, round table where he had a jar of fresh water and an array of paints.

There, he perched, taking up his palette and his brush, and with hunched shoulders that would surely make his back ache, he began to work.

Caroline did her best to concentrate on her own drawing, but she had never had any talent for it, and it was not long before she became distracted by her father's skills. She watched him work, mesmerised, taking in the scene that he was putting onto the stretched canvas with dabs of paint here, elegant strokes and delicate stippling there.

It was a portrait of a family of three—husband, wife, and son—set against a wintry, countryside landscape. They were arranged in front of a towering cedar, the tree holding onto its green needles though the boughs were heavy with snow, and the family were wrapped up warm in fur-trimmed cloaks that gave them a regal air.

How does he do it? Caroline marvelled, wondering how he knew what colours to use and how to turn each brushstroke into something so realistic, the family looking like they might emerge from the canvas at any moment to stretch out stiff limbs from posing for so long.

Meanwhile, at her side on the chaise-longue, Esther was diligently drawing the jug, apple, and spoon. Caroline glanced at it, resisting the urge to laugh; it would have been too unkind. But the jug was too fat and distorted, the spoon too short and strange, the apple closer to resembling a potato.

From the high stool, Adam cleared his throat, having no need to turn around as he said, "Caro, I don't hear your charcoal on the paper."

"Sorry, Papa." She grinned and returned her attention to her task, sticking out her tongue for concentration as she began to draw the three objects in front of her, knowing full-well that she had no hope of capturing them with any skill.

Despite having no talent for drawing, there was something hypnotic and soothing about drawing. Caroline became invested in getting the shape and light right, time running away from her as she obsessed over every line and detail. So much so that she did not notice that her father had stopped working on the canvas and had begun a drawing of his own, turned towards his daughters instead of away from them.

"Papa, what are you doing?" Esther asked, drawing Caroline's attention to the change.

Adam smiled and put a finger to his lips, his gaze flitting from his daughters to the rectangle of paper he had set on a wooden board, balanced on his thighs. The stick of charcoal moved quickly and deftly, both girls stopping what they were doing as they watched him work.

Ten minutes later, he paused and held up the paper.

Etched upon it was an image of Caroline and Esther looking back at him, so detailed and realistic that it stole Caroline's breath away. She would never understand how he could draw like that, and so quickly: if he had been born with that talent or if it had taken countless years of diligent practise.

"It's us!" Esther chirped delightedly.

"It is," Adam replied with a laugh. "As it turns out, I can't work with the two of you here. I suspected as much, so I thought I might as well capture the pair of you distracting me. You're both very noisy when you draw."

Caroline smiled. "Sorry, Papa."

"No reason to apologise." He hopped down off his stool, and took up a thick boar's bristle brush, slicking something across the drawing of his daughters. "We'll leave that to dry, then we'll head back to your mother. I stand a greater chance of working at home than I do here. Now, what do you say to some tea and a story whilst we wait for that paste to dry?"

Caroline and Esther brightened, nodding eagerly. They loved nothing more than to hear their father's stories. Indeed, he was as gifted a storyteller as he was a painter, though Caroline suspected that the two were somehow intertwined: an ability to conjure something out of nothing, creating realistic images on a canvas and in the mind.

Having prepared the tea, Adam came back over with a tray that he set on the low table in front of the chaise-longue, clearing away the jug, apple, and spoon. He sat right down on the floor as he poured a cup for his daughter and himself, and as he handed the cups to the girls, he began: "A long time ago, when dragons were as common in the skies as seagulls and just as likely to steal one's luncheon, there was a squire named Desmond Ramsbottom, who had recently, and rather foolishly, lost his master, Sir Roke…"

* * *

"And though King Desmond was much beloved by his people, he was never quite as happy as he had been as a squire, for he hated responsibility and no one had as much of *that* as a king," Adam concluded with a smile, the paste now dry on the drawing of his daughters.

Caroline applauded in delight. "Another wonderful tale, Papa!"

"One of your best," Esther agreed, grinning.

"I thought so." Adam flashed a wink as he folded up the drawing and handed it to Caroline. "For the two of you. Keep it safe; it might be worth something one day."

Caroline took it gratefully. "I shall guard it with my life."

"Why does Caro get to keep it?" Esther pouted a little, as their father encouraged them to put on their cloaks and hats and gloves.

"It is for both of you," he insisted, "but one of you must bear the responsibility of its safety. Do you want to be like Desmond the squire or King Desmond?"

Esther considered the question. "Desmond the squire. He was happier."

"Exactly, so don't fight and don't pout." Adam laughed softly, donning his own coat and hat. "Come now, your mother will be hungry for her soup."

The trio left the studio, relieved to find that the rain had abated, though the winds had not. They faced it head-on, bent almost diagonal against the gusts as they made the short journey across the piazza to a stall that sold the finest broth in, perhaps, all of London: a perfect cure for a stormy day and a poorly mother.

"You're lucky you caught me," the soup-seller said as Adam gave his order. "I was about to close for the day, before me and all me soup flies away."

Adam laughed. "Now *that's* something I wouldn't mind seeing, if you'll pardon me. The Great Soup Flood of London—you can't deny it has a beauty to it."

"You're a strange one, Mr. Calder," the soup-seller replied with an amused smile, as she ladled the rich, glistening broth into a metal urn. She did not do that for just anyone, but Adam was a regular customer who she knew could be trusted to bring back the vessel.

"You're not the first to say so," he agreed, as he paid and took possession of the delicious soup.

With the goods in hand, Adam and his daughters paused to purchase fresh bread from his favoured bakery, as well as a welcome surprise of candied fruits for the girls, before beginning the reasonably lengthy walk back to the edges of Saint Pancras.

Passing a small row of shops, however, Adam halted again, outside a place that always made Caroline's nose itch. The bitter aroma of herbs and tinctures drifted out into the street, carried by the vicious wind, making her eyes water.

"One more thing," Adam said, stepping into the apothecary.

Caroline and Esther entered the shop behind him, the pungent smells of mysterious brews and medicinal tonics catching in Caroline's throat. She knew that the apothecary was a necessity amongst society, particularly to those who could not afford the talents of a physician, but she had never quite trusted *this* apothecary.

There was something about the man at the counter that reminded her of a bird. More specifically, a vulture.

CHAPTER 4

"I heard they steal toes and pickle them," Esther whispered, eager fingertips reaching for a large brown bottle on one of the bowing shelves to the side of the shop.

Caroline lightly smacked her sister's hand. "Of course they don't pickle toes, you oaf." She stifled a giggle. "Don't touch anything."

"Don't touch anything," their father echoed, approaching the counter and the cold-eyed, beak-nosed, bald-pated apothecary who stood behind it, so still and watchful that Caroline would not have dared put a fingertip on anything in the shop.

Instead, Caroline took her sister's hand and wandered around, observing at a safe distance. There were countless bottles and vials and jars, labelled with names that were beyond Caroline's understanding, or etched with words so tiny that she could not possibly decipher them.

At the same time, Caroline absently listened to what her father was saying to the apothecary, curious to discover if there was a name for the sickness that had been plaguing her mother.

"Anything that might aid with... women's ailments," Adam said in a whisper, as if it was something that should not be mentioned aloud. "She is with-child and has been unwell for some weeks."

The apothecary nodded. "Nothing to be concerned about. I have the very thing."

Satisfied, Caroline returned to her perusal of the shop, and all of its oddities. There *were* strange things in glass jars that, on first look, appeared to be pickled, but none of the objects were toes. Some, however, looked particularly unsettling, like terrifying creatures that had been caught and stuffed into those jars: beings with tentacles and countless arms, insectile in appearance. It took a second look for Caroline to realise, with some relief, that they were just roots and plants and herbs. Nothing strange or nefarious at all, at least not to her untrained eyes.

Just then, the bell above the door jingled. It was a pleasant sound, out of place amidst the peculiarity of the shop.

"Caro?" Esther whispered with a smirk. "What on earth did you do to make that boy despise you so much?"

It took a second for Caroline to realise what her sister was talking about. Quentin had just entered the shop and, at his side, that scowling boy, who seemed no more pleased to be there than he had been at the Sadler's Wells garden.

"Good day to you," Quentin said affably, raising his hand in greeting to the girls.

Caroline bowed her head, offering a polite smile. "And to you, Mr. Rawle."

"A terrible storm we're having, aren't we?" Esther chimed in.

Quentin seemed amused by the grown-up remark. "Yes, terrible indeed. I thought I would be blown away at least twice!"

The boy peered up at the older man with a withering expression that Quentin did not seem to notice. Rather, Quentin pressed on towards the counter, calling out a greeting to Adam as he did so.

"I don't see you for years, and now I've seen you twice in as many days," Quentin said with a grin, clapping Adam on the shoulder.

Caroline did not like the way Quentin kept doing that to her father. It was too familiar, too possessive somehow.

Adam chuckled, standing in such a way that suggested he was trying to hide what he was doing from his old acquaintance. Embarrassed, almost. "London might be a city, but it can feel like a village sometimes," he said. "I hope you're not unwell?"

"Goodness, no," Quentin replied. "I take a daily tonic for vigour and vitality. And you? I hope all is well?"

"The same thing," Adam lied. "It aids with my work."

Quentin nodded, apparently missing the fib. "Yes, your work. I always hoped you would make something of yourself, Calder, and I'm so very pleased to see that you have. In truth, I was going to come by your studio to ask about a commission, but realised I had no notion of where it was. You are long past the days of painting in the corner of our lodgings in Southwark."

"I am," Adam replied cheerily enough. "Though I do miss those days from time to time. There was a... magic to my corner of those lodgings. The light in the evening, coming through that great hole in the roof—I have never been able to replicate it."

Quentin laughed softly. "It was beautiful light. You

should come to my townhouse one evening—the light is *almost* as good." He paused. "When might you be at your studio next, if I feel inclined to come by for that commission? I realise you are terribly busy, but just a sketch from an old friend would be quite enough."

"Tomorrow, I imagine, if the storm permits," Adam replied, gesturing out to the street where an elderly couple battled to keep possession of their hats, and a large piece of fabric that resembled a sail whipped by, dragged by the wind. "Alas, my commissions don't care if the weather is bad; they must be finished. I am ordinarily at my studio from Monday to Saturday—nine o'clock until three o'clock, longer of a Saturday. It would be my pleasure to have you come by, to see how much has changed."

A sharp elbow caught Caroline in the arm, a curt voice reprimanding, "No one ever tell you it's rude to eavesdrop? That isn't your conversation to be part of."

She gasped in fright, wondering how Luke had crept up on her with such stealth. Her alarm swiftly transformed into annoyance at his accusation, though she could not exactly defend herself; she *had* been eavesdropping, and rather obviously too.

"Don't presume to touch me," she muttered, dusting off her arm where he had nudged her harshly. "And don't presume to know what conversations I should and shouldn't be privy to. You mind your own business."

Luke shrugged, eyeing her with less ferocity than before, his grey eyes taking on a gleam of curiosity. "Mr. Rawle doesn't like anyone knowing his business is all. Heed my warning or don't—it doesn't matter to me."

"Has anyone ever told *you* that you're a very rude young man?" Caroline shot back, glancing around to try and figure out where Esther had gone.

THE CHILD SHE NEVER SPOKE OF

The younger girl was crouched down, inspecting some of the dusty jars on the lowest shelves, where more of those roots and plants were held prisoner in mysterious, viscous liquids.

Luke snorted. "Rude for telling you not to listen in on conversations that aren't for your ears? You've got some high-and-mighty notions, Miss Calder." He puffed up a breath, blowing a wavy lock of golden hair out of his eye. "As I say, heed my warning or don't. Just trying to keep you from getting a worse scolding."

"He's my father," Caroline protested. "Whatever he says, I can listen to."

Lifting his shoulders in another infuriating shrug, Luke flashed a cold smile. "Suit yourself."

The boy turned and strode out of the shop, the bell above the door not sounding nearly as pleasant upon his departure. Caroline followed the boy's movements out onto the street, where he paused and breathed in the stormy air for a second, before wandering out of view.

Returning her gaze to her father and Quentin, she flinched inwardly. Quentin's attention had been captured by the jingle of the bell, and he did not look best pleased that his nephew had just walked out without saying a word. A flare of anger flashed in his grey eyes, extinguished quickly as Adam said something to him.

"I can see the apothecary is occupied, and I am in something of a hurry," Quentin said. "I'll come to visit you soon. Give my well wishes to your dear wife."

Setting his hat back on his head, the strange, overly familiar man marched to the door and out into the street, staring this way and that with an expression that reminded Caroline of a predator who had lost the scent of its prey, infuriated by the lack. After a moment, he stalked off in the direction that Luke had gone and, for a fleeting and inexplicable instant, Caroline hoped that he would not catch up to the boy.

I am being ridiculous... She shook off the feeling and went to heave Esther to her feet. *Just because the man is odd does not mean he is nefarious, and that boy* is *an irksome creature. I would probably be annoyed too if he walked off when he was not supposed to.*

After all, Quentin was one of Adam's oldest friends, having resided together for years in their youth. If her father did not think there was anything amiss with his acquaintance, then Caroline had no reason to either.

"Apologies for the delay," the apothecary said, returning from the back room where he had disappeared to, carrying something tightly wrapped in brown paper. "This ought to help your wife."

Adam took the package gratefully. "Thank you."

"Six drops, no more than three times a day should suffice," the apothecary instructed.

Adam nodded and thanked the man again, expelling what looked like a breath of relief. "Come on, girls. Let's get home to your mother."

As they left the apothecary, Caroline stole a glance at the brown paper, twisted around what might have been a small bottle or a vial. The bitter scent of the shop clung to her nostrils, her stomach somewhat queasy as she drank in the fresh and violent air.

"What medicine is that?" she dared to ask as they walked towards home.

Adam smiled. "Just medicine so your mother doesn't feel so poorly anymore."

"Is it the baby making her poorly?"

Adam frowned, nodding a little. "It is not unusual. Nothing to worry about. She was the same with the two of you." He brightened, grasping the brown paper package a little tighter. "But this will help. Now, my little ducks, hurry yourselves before this soup gets cold."

CHAPTER 5

Heather was awake when Caroline, her sister, and her father stepped through the front door of their Saint Pancras apartments, struck by the heat and comfort that radiated through every room and hallway. It was a sanctuary away from the terrible storm raging outside: a bubble of peace and contentment where they could sequester themselves.

"Is it so late in the day already?" Heather asked from the small table in the kitchen, the thin skin around her eyes speckled with little reddish dots that had not been there when everyone departed that morning. The sign of strain, brought on by the baby sickness.

Adam set down the urn of soup and went to put his arms around his wife, kissing the top of her auburn hair. "The school was closed due to the storm, and I couldn't work with my two darling daughters distracting me." He bent his head and kissed her cheek. "We thought we would bring you soup and keep you company instead."

"Goodness, I'm relieved." Heather mustered a tired laugh. "I thought I'd lost an entire day!"

She had a cup of tea in front of her, mostly untouched, and still wore her nightgown and housecoat. It was curious for Caroline to behold, for she had never known her mother to be anything but immaculately dressed and groomed for the day ahead. In truth, her mother looked so much younger, her hair loose and tousled, her skin smooth and pale.

"How are you feeling?" Adam asked, leaving his wife for a moment to fetch bowls and spoons for the soup, and some of the fresh bread that sat on a nearby counter.

Heather smiled thinly. "Well enough. I suppose I forgot what it was actually like to be with-child. You... put certain things out of your mind after a while, and I am experiencing a harsh reminder." She leaned into Adam as he came to hold her again. "But I am grateful we are where we are, this time. Do you remember, with Caro, when I had my head in that rusty old bucket for a week?"

Adam chuckled, rocking his wife gently. "How could I forget? I remember Mrs. O'Rourke holding your hair back and feeding you little pieces of that bread she used to make."

"I wouldn't have survived it without her," Heather agreed with a sad sigh. "I've thought of her often these past weeks."

Esther held out her bowl as Caroline moved to pour the soup from the urn. "Who is Mrs. O'Rourke?" the younger girl asked, licking her lips as the aroma of the rich broth wafted upwards, filling the small kitchen.

"She was a lady who lived where we did," Heather said haltingly, as if the memory was too great. "Came over from Ireland with her son. She took care of me though she didn't have to, and... we never had the opportunity to repay that favour."

Caroline passed a bowl of broth to her mother. "What do you mean?"

"She died not long after you were born," Adam interjected gently. "Consumption or something like it. I don't know where her son went afterwards, but I hope he found a good life for himself."

Heather took up her spoon, dipping it into the broth. "She taught me so much about motherhood and pregnancy." Her voice caught in her throat. "I can't bear it when I see people saying such unkind things about the Irish in the papers, in the streets, wherever I go. There were many who lived where we did, back then, and I trusted every last one. There was such life in those lodgings, such care, such..."

She brought the spoon to her mouth and sipped, closing her eyes with a frown, as if she did not know if it was going to make her worse or better. Her throat bobbed as she swallowed the soup, and when her eyes opened again, they were watery.

"I wish you could have met her," she said quietly, going back for another spoonful.

Caroline tried to imagine such a woman, taking care of her mother in dismal lodgings that were a far cry from the nice apartments they now enjoyed. She tried to imagine her father being a penniless artist with nothing but desperation to motivate him. But it was near impossible for Caroline, who could not remember such times, to think of a life that was any different to the one they had now.

"Was Quentin there?" Caroline asked suddenly.

Adam quirked an eyebrow. "No, he had returned to his father's house by then, to join the family business. I *do* remember that he used to say that I was mad not to do the same, or to find some other trade, after I married your mother." He smiled and leaned over to kiss Heather. "He never understood that your mother was as mad as I was, *believed* in my work as much as I did—more, most likely."

"I'd have raised you both in those lodgings if I'd had to," Heather agreed, a hint of colour coming back into her cheeks.

Esther pulled a face at that, though she did not say anything as she dipped bread into her broth and ate the soggy pieces with obvious delight. After all, she knew even less about the struggles that their mother and father had endured to get to where they were now. She had been born and raised in the upper-middle class and clearly did not like the idea of a different scenario.

After another spoonful or three, the colour in Heather's cheeks blanched again, her hand pressed to her stomach as a funny, uncomfortable expression rippled across her pale face.

Seeing it at the same time as Caroline, Adam reached for the brown paper package and took out the contents. "I visited the apothecary," he said by way of explanation. "The man said this would help you."

He went to fetch two spoons, popping the stopper out of a brown glass bottle. He poured a measure onto the spoon and, very carefully, deposited six droplets from that spoon to another, before tipping what was left back into the bottle. It could not have been cheap, though Caroline had not thought to eavesdrop on the price of the medicine.

"What is it?" Heather sniffed the liquid, her nose wrinkling at the scent.

Caroline also sniffed the air, catching the faint whiff of something strange—a musky, earthy aroma with notes of untanned leather and horses. Not pleasant, but not unpleasant. Certainly not the sort of medicinal scent she would have expected.

THE CHILD SHE NEVER SPOKE OF

"Medicine, love," Adam replied, feeding her the dose.

Heather grimaced as she swallowed the mixture, sticking out her tongue as if she wanted the air to take away the flavour. She shuddered and followed the medicine with a spoonful of broth.

"I love you dearly," she said to her husband, "but that is vile. It has a greater chance of making me feel *more* unwell."

Adam chuckled. "The more bitter the medicine..."

"The better it is for you," Caroline and Esther chorused in unison, the former hoping with all of her heart that the unusual-smelling liquid would help her mother.

And as the minutes went by, the family enjoying their unexpected luncheon together, it seemed that the medicine *was* working upon Heather. She savoured each mouthful of the broth, closing her eyes in delight as if it were the most delicious thing she had ever tasted, and when her eyes opened again, there was a giddiness in her gaze. The kind of expression that Caroline had only seen in her mother a few times before, on special occasions, after a few glasses of gifted wine.

Presently, Heather began to sway in her chair, laughing softly to herself.

"Love?" Adam quirked an eyebrow, taking hold of her hand.

"I feel as if I could fly," Heather sighed, smiling so wide that all of Caroline's worries faded away. Her mother was feeling better. Her mother was feeling wonderful, in fact, some colour coming back into her cheeks, her eyes bright, if slightly glazed.

"You must dance with me, darling," Heather said urgently, getting to her feet, pulling Adam up with her.

Adam laughed. "There's no music, my love."

"We don't need music." She stepped closer to him with

such adoration in her eyes, looping her arms around her husband's neck.

Never one to deny his wife a dance, Adam slipped his arms around Heather's waist and, together, they swayed to music only they could hear in the small kitchen of those Saint Pancras apartments. Caroline looked at the scene, her heart so full she feared it might burst, clapping along to give them some manner of rhythm—though it did not seem like they needed it.

"Girls, come and dance!" Heather cried, opening out her arm and beckoning for her daughters to join in.

Esther ran into the embrace, while Caroline was slower, shyer to join in with the odd dance. But as her mother and father pulled her into a circle, arms entangled, faces smiling, feet tripping over everyone else's, she could not help but feel the giddy spirit that had taken hold of her mother. It was contagious and glorious, making her feel like it was her birthday again, as they swayed and jigged and tried not to bump into the table or the counters.

"Is this not far better than school?" Esther chirped, giggling merrily as they hopped around in a circle. "I hope we never have to go back!"

Just then, as if summoned, there *was* music. A jaunty tune drifting up to the sash windows from the inn at the bottom of the road: fiddles and flutes and drums, conjuring the most beautiful song that Caroline had ever heard, for it was entirely perfect, adding the missing piece to the joyous moment.

"Is this real?" Caroline gasped, grinning as the dancing quickened, all four of them whirling around and around, holding onto each other for dear life.

"Of course it is, darling!" Heather cried, closing her eyes as she let the rhythm and the dance and the music carry her, with such peace on her face that it felt like magic to Caroline. A magic that crackled in the air, so wild and wonderful that Caroline wished she could grab it and bottle it, for that would surely be the greatest medicine of them all.

As the dizzying dance began to make Caroline's head swim, her lungs straining for breath, she wondered if she was being given a second chance to make the wish that she had not finished the other night. Why else would it feel like there was magic in the air? Why else would it feel as if a wish was being demanded?

I wish for life to feel like this—to feel like a dream. The words came to her mind unbidden, seeming so *right*, so appropriate, so perfect, that she knew she must be right: she *had* been given a second chance to make her birthday wish. And as she danced and danced with her family, overcome with love for them, she could not have imagined that some force beyond her control—beyond anyone's control—might twist her wish into the very opposite of what her heart wanted.

Indeed, what she could not have known, in that glorious moment, was that dreams could often turn into nightmares without warning.

CHAPTER 6

"I think you wished too hard," Caroline remarked to Esther, as they stared out of the parlour window at the vicious weather that still held London in its Arctic grip.

The ferocious winds and driving rains had cooled, the temperatures dropping to the bitterest that Caroline could remember, certainly for January. Outside, a blizzard had turned the world a blurry white, snow lying thick on the cobbles and pavements and stretches of grass that had undoubtedly thought they had seen their last freeze and thaw of winter. The plane trees and sycamores bent and groaned in the winds that had not abated, shaking the snow free of their boughs, protesting with each creaking branch.

"Long may it last," Esther replied cheerily, returning to the book in her hand.

Caroline pulled a disapproving face, for although she had enjoyed the additional few days with her family, she was starting to become restless. Unlike her sister, she adored her education, striving to do well under Frances

Buss's watchful eye, determined to make the most of the privilege that she had been granted. But even if there was no terrible storm outside, she would have had nowhere to go, for it was Saturday—a day she usually looked forward to but now felt endless.

Just then, Adam wandered into the room, resting his hands on his hips as his narrowed eyes surveyed the parlour.

"They are underneath the red cushion," Caroline said, stifling a laugh.

Her father's expression relaxed as he went to the settee and plucked up the cushion to find a long pouch underneath. "Thank you, darling."

He retrieved the pouch, containing some of his best brushes, and tucked the folded leather into the lapel of his waistcoat.

Caroline frowned. "You're not going to the studio in this, are you?"

"I can't delay any longer," he replied with an apologetic shrug. "Mr. Liddell is expecting delivery of the portrait on Wednesday, and it is not at all finished. It is *Mrs.* Liddell's birthday on Friday, and as it is meant to be a gift, it must be done." He ran an anxious hand through his fair hair, greying at the sides. "I shouldn't have left it so late."

Caroline saw her opportunity and seized it. "I'll come with you."

"You'll do no such thing," her father replied, gesturing to the window. "You should stay inside where it's warm, and where you can be near to your mother in case she needs anything."

"Esther can tend to Mama," Caroline insisted. "I have two books that I need to read, and I can't concentrate here. Please, Papa, let me come with you. I'll be as quiet as a mouse and I'll tend to the fire so that neither of us get cold, and I'll make luncheon for us both and anything else that you need. I'll—"

"Keep chattering like a magpie until you get your way?" Adam interrupted with a sigh that was somehow both weary and amused.

Caroline blushed, knowing it was uncharacteristic of her to be so demanding. But, truly, she could not bear another moment within the same walls, slowly losing her mind.

"I'll worry about you otherwise," she said quietly.

Adam puffed out a breath, glancing from his daughter to the snowflakes that exploded against the windowpane. He probably thought she was mad for wanting to give up the warmth of the apartments for the biting blizzard, but his faint shrug gave her all the encouragement she needed.

"Very well, but I don't want to hear any complaints that it's too cold," her father warned. "And you're not to make a peep whilst I work, or I'll bring you right back and I won't be pleased about it."

Caroline nodded effusively. "I promise, I won't disturb you a bit."

"Esther, take care of your mother whilst we're away. Make sure she has her medicine when she needs it," Adam ordered. "And you, my dear, quite mad Caro, put on your warmest clothes and be at the front door in ten minutes."

Esther looked up from her book. "I will, Papa. I shall relish the heat by the fire whilst you both freeze yourselves." She tutted under her breath. "Make sure you don't catch your death out there."

"You mean, you can't be persuaded to come with us?" Adam asked with a glint of mischief in his eyes.

Esther raised an eyebrow at him. "I can think of nothing

worse. No, I daresay I shall stay here and read my book to Mama."

It was something the girls did often, reading stories to their mother, for though they were literate, their mother was not. It was, perhaps, one of the reasons why Heather was so adamant that her own daughters should be educated in a way that she had never had the opportunity to be.

"Last chance to change your mind," Adam said, smiling.

Esther returned her attention to her book. "Enjoy yourselves. Think of me when you are shivering, and your hands are too numb to even hold a cup of tea."

Laughing, Adam turned to leave, calling out, "Ten minutes, Caro!" as he headed out of the parlour with his brushes safely tucked into his waistcoat.

* * *

IT TOOK five minutes for Caroline to regret her decision to go to the studio with her father, as snowflakes whipped at her face and stung her cheeks with shards of ice. She wrapped her scarf tighter and higher up her face, her hot breath soaking through the wool, but it was no good; the wind and snow managed to sneak through, biting harder in vengeance against the attempt to keep it at bay.

Her feet were frozen solid, trudging through the snow that seeped through her shoes, her hat kept threatening to blow away, and her gloves were entirely useless against a cold so absolute. Her thick woollen cloak, too.

Just then, her father began to sing, smiling above the top edge of his scarf. A song that Caroline vaguely knew, though it had not been around for very long.

"All things bright and beautiful..." His rich tenor greeted her ears, a balm to her discomfort.

"All creatures great and small," she sang back.

"All things wise and wonderful..."

"The Lord God made them all."

It appeared that their mutual knowledge of the lyrics ended there, though that did not stop her father. He chuckled as he made up the next verse, joking about the storm and 'every mean little snowflake' before they joined in together for the chorus, singing loud and with all the merriment they could muster, chasing away the unpleasant weather minute by minute.

They continued on like that, taking turns to make up the verses, leaping into the chorus with greater and greater enthusiasm, until Caroline had all but forgotten how viciously cold it was. It also seemed to quicken time itself, as familiar sights shifted through the haze of endless white, appearing and disappearing, letting the pair know that they would soon reach Covent Garden.

"All things bright and beautiful!" Caroline sang with all her might, as they came to the last road before the piazza.

"All creatures great and small!" her father replied with aplomb.

"All things wise and wonderful!" She hesitated, peering through the veil of strafing snow. Her eyes watered, making the visibility twice as awful, prompting her to stand still for a moment to try and rub the blur away.

Her father stepped out into the road and turned around to look at her, splaying out his arms like he was upon the stage in the Royal Opera House, *"The Lord God made—"*

As she walked forward to join in with him, a terrifying sound drowned out the last words: the thunderous beat of hooves, coming from the left. Caroline could see nothing, the blizzard making it seem as if the noise was coming from everywhere and nowhere, all at once. Ghost horses stampeding through the streets, for no real horse would deign to be out in such appalling weather.

A vast, dark smudge appeared in the frothing white. Caroline had enough time to see the faint gleam of lanterns, too feeble to make any difference in the vicious storm, before an almighty blow caught her in the chest, sending her flying backwards. The impact of two solid palms throbbed against her ribs. Her father had shoved her; she knew that much, but as she sailed backwards and her head struck the snowy ground, all thoughts jolted out of her mind.

She lay there, dazed, as the snow continued to streak downward. Staring upwards, the world was strange, like a million pinpricks in a swathe of dark grey velvet.

Where am I? Is this still London?

All of a sudden, a rough hand caught her around the arm and hauled her to her feet. A dark figure, face obscured by the snow and the dizziness that pulsed in Caroline's eyes.

"I'm sorry," a gruff voice rasped, the grip on her arm releasing. "I'm so sorry."

Then, she was alone again, the figure merging back into the blizzard. She heard the faint rattle of a carriage and the muted thud of hoofbeats, but could not decide what was real and what was in her mind.

Her head hurt, temples throbbing, as she blinked through the blinding haze of the blizzard, remembering that her father was somewhere nearby. He had shoved her, and then... What had happened?

"Papa?" she shouted, taking a step forward that nearly downed her again.

A sharp pain splintered up her leg, her ankle protesting.

"Papa?" she called again, more desperately.

Gritting her teeth, she hobbled out into the road, squinting this way and that for any sign of her father.

"Papa, where are—"

She saw it, illuminated beneath the wobbly amber glow of a streetlamp, spreading quickly across the thick blanket of settled snow: a pool of vivid red, soaking through that endless white. And at the very edge of that fuzzy circle of light: a fallen figure, a long leather pouch on the ground beside him, spilling brushes towards the gutter, the bristles coated in that awful, terrible scarlet.

CHAPTER 7

Caroline sat in the gloom of the parlour, greyish dawn light hardly daring to peek in through the curtains, as if it knew it was not welcome; that it should not dare to intrude on the cloistered realm of the Calder household. A cup of tea had gone cold in Caroline's hands, untouched and untasted.

Down the hallway, the first whimpers of keening distress that would provide the accompaniment to the rest of the day, stemmed solely by a spoonful of strange medicine.

"Caro!" came the customary wail that had plagued Caroline for a fortnight. "Caro, please! My medicine!"

Caroline squeezed her eyes shut, wishing that everything would return to the way it had been when she opened them again. *It's all a mistake. A wretched mistake. Papa is going to walk into the parlour searching for his charcoal or his brushes, and I'll joke that he needs to tether them to himself. Papa is going to carry Mama into the room and set her down on the settee, and he'll kiss her and then usher us all out to school. Any moment now, he'll come back...*

"Caro!" her mother called in desperation.

"He has to come back," Caroline whispered, her eyes still scrunched.

A world without her father was an impossibility. She could not think of another person who so encompassed what it was to be alive, so how could it be that he... was *not* anymore? He had been so bright, so cheerful, so lively; his work so famous and beloved that it could not simply *end* with an unfinished portrait in the studio. He had so much more to do. He had a third child to meet and adore. He had two daughters to watch grow, and to set an example for of what marriage should look like, lavishing love and attention on their mother.

She can't survive without him. None of us can.

"Caro, please! Caro, bring me my medicine!" Anger laced the sorrow of Heather's voice, her shouts getting louder.

She did not—and did not want to—exist between doses of that bitter medicine. The past two weeks had proven that. She would not get out of bed, she barely ate anything, barely drank anything, and had been asking for more and more of her medicine.

Deep down, something told Caroline that she should not give in to her mother's increasingly insistent pleas, but she could not be the one who allowed her mother to suffer, either. Whenever Heather asked for the medicine, Caroline gave it, no matter how reluctantly. Here and there, she had even been tempted to take some herself, to see if it would help her own pain, but *that*, at least, she had managed to resist.

"Caro!" her mother shrieked.

Caroline opened her eyes and took a breath. "Coming, Mama."

She grabbed the offending brown bottle and two spoons from the little kitchen, and went to the dingy bedchamber that her mother refused to leave. The curtains were drawn, the linens had not been laundered, and last night's dinner sat cold and congealed and untouched on the bedside table.

"What took you so long?" her mother hissed, sitting up in the dark like a creature of the underworld: pale and drawn and bony, her nightgown loose and discoloured with a fortnight of wear, her eyes feverish and black in the low light.

"I couldn't find a second spoon," Caroline lied, coming to perch on the edge of her mother's bed.

The other side of the bed was jarringly neat, the sheets tucked, the pillows plumped, the coverlets undisturbed, so it would be ready for Adam to slip back into when he returned from wherever he had gone.

"The bottle is almost empty," Caroline said hesitantly as she poured a measure onto the spoon and dripped six drops onto another.

Heather stared at the spoon with a madness that unnerved Caroline. "Then, get some more. Your father has money in his study. Take whatever you need; he won't mind."

She had not yet spoken of her husband in the past tense, not realising that the pretence only made it harder for Caroline and her sister to come to terms with what had happened. If Heather could not believe it, how could her daughters?

"A few more drops, if you please," Heather murmured, her voice hazy as though speaking through fog. "Just a little more—it helps settle the nerves.

cCaroline hesitated and pretended to add two more drops. "Here you go."

She fed her mother the spoonful, grimacing as she watched her mother drink it down greedily, licking the curve of the spoon to ensure she got every morsel. Once she had, she wriggled back down beneath the dirty coverlets and closed her eyes, expelling a contented sigh.

I shouldn't give her any more... Caroline no longer liked what the medicine did to her mother. Where before it had made her cheerful and giddy, now it made her blank-eyed and slightly mad, ranting and raving until she got her next dose. In-between, all she did was sleep.

Although, Caroline could not be sure if the reaction was actually due to the medicine or if it was merely grief, corrupting and corroding the woman that she had known, all of her life, as 'Mama.' Until she could figure that out, Caroline would keep giving her mother the medicine, regardless of how much she hated it.

"I'll sleep now," Heather murmured. "Your father is waiting for me."

She turned over, showing her bony back to Caroline, dismissing her daughter without saying a word. Caroline had done her job; she did not need to linger past her purpose.

Putting the stopper back into the bottle, Caroline retreated from the bedchamber and padded down the hallway, back to the parlour. Her mother would undoubtedly sleep for hours now, meaning countless empty hours now stretched before Caroline.

So, she was not expecting someone else to already be in the parlour.

"Esther!" Caroline gasped, her hand flying to her chest. "You scared me half to death!"

The younger girl turned mournful, tired eyes towards Caroline, a hint of accusation in them. "Don't say that."

"Sorry, Estie," Caroline said more gently. "It's just a turn of phrase. I meant nothing by it."

Esther nodded, sniffing. "Is Mama asleep again?"

"She is."

Esther nodded again, like her head did not know what else to do. "Can we go to Papa's grave today? It doesn't look like it will rain."

"Not today," Caroline replied, sitting down close to her sister on the settee.

Esther chewed her lower lip. "Is it... bad if someone isn't buried yet? Will it stop him... from being allowed to enter... Heaven?"

"Not at all, Estie." Caroline reached for her sister's hand, holding it tightly. "The priest came to the mortuary. Papa's soul is... free to enter Heaven. And his body will be safe in the mortuary until the ground is fit for his burial. The undertaker said he would send word—I doubt it will be much longer."

The January storms had added insult to the injury of Adam Calder's departure from the mortal world; the snow and ice making the ground too hard to dig any sort of grave. And when the last breath of winter had thawed and melted, the ground became so oversaturated that any attempt at digging a hole resulted in a deep pool of water that no casket deserved to be submerged in. As such, the girls' father was being kept at the mortuary, at great expense, though it was not the money that Caroline cared about; *she* could not bear to think of him so cold and alone in that awful place, with no one to hold his hand or put an extra blanket over him.

He looked like he was sleeping. His face was peaceful. He

didn't seem to be in any pain. She kept wanting to tell Esther of what she had witnessed at that unfeeling, stark mortuary, when she had made that wretched journey with her father, but she doubted it would do any good. It could not even comfort her.

"I wish I had gone with you," Esther mumbled, tugging at a loose thread in the seam of her skirts. "I think I'll always regret not going with you that day."

Caroline squeezed Esther's hand. "Papa wouldn't have wanted that. He'll have thought of you, warm and safe at home with your book, and I know that would have made him happy."

I wish I hadn't gone with him... Caroline held her tongue, for being there in her father's last moments was one of the most bittersweet events of her life. A constant conflict in her mind between gratitude and regret. Yes, she had held him as he took his final breath, and yes, she also wished that responsibility had *not* fallen on her, for she would never be able to rid herself of the image. The silence that had followed. So absolute.

"Are you sure he didn't say anything when he died?" Esther murmured.

Caroline nodded. "He just looked at me."

He had not possessed the strength to speak, though Caroline had spoken enough for the both of them, begging him not to leave his family, telling him over and over how much he was loved, promising to be a better daughter if he would just hold on.

"I miss him." Esther's voice caught in her throat and, all of a sudden, she was in Caroline's arms, sobbing into her older sister's chest.

Caroline held her close, stroking her hair, whispering

soothing things, letting Esther get it all out. It served no one any favours to hold such things inside.

Weirdly, Caroline had not cried yet. She had tried, worried that something might be wrong with her, but tears would not come. There was grief, there was sorrow, there was all-consuming dread about the future, but it was like the shock of it all had blocked the channels that allowed tears to fall.

I have to keep everyone else afloat first. She could still hear the singular, animal scream that her mother had made when she had come home from the mortuary, forced to tell the rest of her family what had happened. A similar scream roared and raged inside Caroline, but it had no means to get out. Not yet. Not until she knew that everyone she loved would be all right.

"You go on back to bed," Caroline said softly, giving Esther a tender squeeze. "I'll bring you some tea and toast, and you can rest or read for a while."

Esther sniffed and smeared her nose on the back of her sleeve. "Can I have lots of butter?"

"Of course." Caroline forced a smile and let go of her sister, leading her out of the parlour and up the hallway to the bedchamber that they had been sharing for the past fortnight. They had tried sleeping alone, but neither wanted the solitude, finding comfort in waking up to hear the breath and sleepy movements of someone else in the room.

Once Esther was tucked up in bed, looking so sad and vulnerable that it broke Caroline's heart afresh, Caroline went to prepare the promised tea and toast. The kitchen was the most consoling part of the house, being too small to ever feel like someone was missing; the memories of that room too joyful to be tarnished by what had happened.

As Caroline made the tea and toast, she pictured her mother and father dancing in the small space behind the table, whilst music floated up from the inn down the road. She vividly remembered joining in with the dance, and how happy they had all been. She remembered endless dinners, filled with laughter and chatter. She remembered her father's attempt to bake a cake for her mother's birthday; the end result so deflated and burnt that her father had, in a desperate panic, hurried to the nearest bakery, which had only had one cake left—so expensive that Adam had practically winced when he had cut into it.

"That's five premium oil paints," he had lamented, biting into his slice.

"I miss you," Caroline whispered, scraping butter onto the thick, stove-toasted bread. She still could not get the colour as perfect as her father used to, but at least she was not burning pieces anymore.

Arranging the tea and toast on a tray, Caroline took it to her sister... and paused in the doorway of the bedchamber. Esther lay curled up beneath the coverlets, her loose, strawberry-blonde hair draped across the pillow, one hand tucked under her cheek, fast asleep. She looked so peaceful that Caroline did not have the heart to disturb her.

I'll make you more later, Caroline promised, carefully tiptoeing backwards, retreating to the parlour to pick at the food and drink. She did not want anything to go to waste, but she did not have the stomach for much.

Pushing aside the tray, she took out a square of paper and the pouch of charcoals that her father had given to her years ago, in the hopes—presumably—that she would prove to be a gifted artist too.

Closing her eyes, she tried to picture her father's face.

She saw his golden-brown eyes, so similar to her own, and the fair hair that could be dark blonde or lightest brown, depending on how the light hit it. Caroline had inherited her mother's auburn hair, while Esther was a blend of both. She imagined the dimple in his chin and the stubble that he was always being reminded to shave; the smiling mouth, the slightly crooked nose gained after a brawl in his youth.

With a breath, focussing intently on the paper, Caroline began to draw. She wanted to capture what was in her head, so that she would never forget what her beloved father looked like. There would be nothing worse than having his memory fade; she was certain of that.

The more she tried to draw him, the more frustrated she became, snapping at least two sticks of charcoal as she desperately tried to coax her memories onto the paper. But whatever artistic talent she possessed had not been honed enough; she could not capture him properly. She could not capture him at all, his likeness all wrong, like seeing a reflection in restless water.

She had just cut another square of paper to start again, when a bell jingled loudly down the hall, frightening her out of her frustration. She gasped in a breath, realising that someone must be downstairs, pulling on the bell for the Calder residence.

I suppose it was only a matter of time... News of Adam's death had made it to the front page of the London papers, and considering his fame, Caroline had been wondering when well-wishers and mourners might start to appear. Although, she had not known they would visit his actual *home*. His studio would have been more appropriate.

Standing up and removing her apron, smoothing out the front of her dress, Caroline headed up the hallway to answer the door. She paused halfway up, squinting at the front door of the apartments. It stood open, as if someone else had already gone out to answer the main door.

Did I leave it open? She did not remember doing so, but then, she had not exactly been herself of late.

Hurrying the rest of the way, she had just made it to the landing when she heard voices down below. Familiar voices. One male, one female.

"I am sorry I have not visited sooner," Quentin said. "I did not think it would be appropriate—you have been through so much, Mrs. Calder. I thought it best to give you all time to grieve in private."

"You are too kind, Mr. Rawle. Goodness, I can't tell you how nice it is to see a friendly face—someone who knew my love," Caroline's mother replied. "Won't you come in for some tea?"

Caroline leaned over the banister, unable to believe that her mother had somehow dragged herself from her medicine-induced stupor and made it to the main door before her. Nor did Heather sound as addled as usual, though there was no denying the impropriety of Heather answering the door in nothing but her nightgown and housecoat.

What are you doing, Mama? Don't invite him in for tea! Caroline wanted to shout, but she held her tongue. Perhaps, seeing a friend of Adam's *would* be good for Heather.

"Are you certain this is not a bad time?" Quentin asked.

"Not at all," Heather replied. "You can wait in the parlour whilst I make myself presentable. Then, we shall have tea."

Quentin nodded. "If you insist, I shall not argue."

Caroline stole one last peek as Quentin entered the main hallway of the building, remembering the boy, Luke, who had given her a warning the last time they had seen one another. A warning that Quentin did not like others knowing his business and would not take kindly to eavesdroppers.

But Luke was not there. Perhaps, after that day in the apothecary, Quentin never *did* catch up to him.

CHAPTER 8

"Caro! Caro, where are you?"

Caroline had been waiting for her mother to call for her, yet she was not certain if she should answer. Quentin Rawle had no business being in their apartments to offer his sympathies, not without some manner of chaperone, and certainly not with Heather in such a fragile condition.

"Caro!" her mother called again, more insistently. "We have a visitor!"

I am aware. Grumbling under her breath, Caroline stepped out of the kitchen as if she had been there all along. Her mother was just emerging from her bedchamber in a simple day dress, her hair tied up with a ribbon, looking far more respectable than she had in two weeks.

"There you are." Heather smiled, though it had a dazed quality. "Might you bring a tea tray for me and Mr. Rawle? We will be in the parlour."

Caroline hesitated. "I'll join you."

"I don't think that would be appropriate, darling," her

mother replied apologetically. "Stay with your sister; I shall summon you if you are needed."

Caroline wanted to protest, but her mother had already drifted off into the parlour, the door closing behind her. Muffled voices filtered out into the hallway, and despite remembering Luke's warning, Caroline promptly rushed off to prepare the tea tray—if only to get closer to whatever was being said in that room.

It can hardly be deemed eavesdropping if I've been asked to fetch tea now, can it?

The kitchen nudged up against the wall of the parlour, and through a crack that damp had opened up that had never been repaired, it was rather easy to hear whatever was going on in the room beyond. Something Caroline's mother had either forgotten, or was counting on, though Caroline had a feeling it was the former.

"I simply cannot understand it," Quentin began, as Caroline squinted through the crack in the wall, wanting to see as well as hear what was going on.

The man stood by the window, looking out onto the street, but he turned as Heather sat down on the settee. He offered her a sad smile and moved away from the window, pausing halfway between the pane and Caroline's mother.

"It does not make sense, does it, that he should be gone, and we are still here?" he continued, his voice thick. "He was the very best of us. As I mentioned, I had intended to visit you sooner, but I did not think that my presence would be appreciated until some time had passed."

Heather looked, for a moment, like she might cry. "It is a comfort to see anyone who was dear to my Adam. You would have been welcome, Mr. Rawle."

"I heard that he was not yet buried." Quentin cleared his throat. "I was sorrier still to hear that. Indeed, when you receive word that he can be buried, I would like to pay for the funeral. It is the very least that I can do for such a dear friend. Goodness, I shall miss him terribly. I know we did not see one another as often as we did in our youth, but I was just getting reacquainted; it seems too cruel."

Heather stared at him, wide-eyed, shaking her head slowly. "That will not be necessary, Mr. Rawle. I could not ask you to pay for his funeral. There is... money set aside, and..." Her breath caught, her chin dipping to her chest, her shoulders shaking as the weight of her new circumstances visibly struck her at once. "We... shall manage."

I hope you are right, Mama. Caroline's heart ached as she watched her mother, wishing fervently that she could run to her and embrace her and sob with her. It was the first time in a fortnight that she had heard something like acceptance from her mother. Resignation, at the very least, to their sorrowful situation. It *had* to be progress. Perhaps, having Quentin visit had been a good idea after all. Perhaps, after this, Heather would not take so much medicine, and might emerge from her bedchamber from time to time. Caroline hoped so.

"Forgive me, Mrs. Calder, but I do not see how you can," Quentin replied in a gentler tone, moving a little closer. "It pains me to think of the situation that you will be left in. Indeed, it is what compelled me to visit, though it is all still so... fresh."

Heather's glassy gaze snapped up to meet his. "What do you mean? I am... certain that my husband has made provisions for us."

Yes, Mama. You tell him, Caroline urged, for there was no way that her father had not taken pains to ensure that his family would be taken care of in the event of his... absence.

"No matter what provisions he has made, dear Mrs.

Calder, it will not be enough," Quentin replied. "I am only saying this because you are the wife of one of my dearest friends, so please do not be cross. I want you and your girls to be well taken care of, that is all, just as I know Adam would have wanted the same."

Heather's throat bobbed. "You are scaring me, Mr. Rawle."

He was scaring Caroline, too.

"I do not mean to," Quentin urged, sitting down in the armchair that was once Adam's favourite. "But there will come a time, sooner than you think, where the money will run dry. You will lose these fine apartments, you will have to work, your daughters will have to work, and all that Adam built for the three of you will crumble. It will be the old days once more."

"No…" Heather gasped, what little colour she had in her face blanching to a ghastly pale.

Quentin nodded slowly. "I am sorry. I am sorry but it is the truth, and I cannot bear it. Yet, it is the only way you will be able to survive if something is not done, and done quickly."

"What can be done?" Heather gasped, a sob strangling the end of her sentence.

She stood sharply, swaying on unsteady feet as her hands clasped together, her eyes wide and wild and imploring as tears trickled down her cheeks. She heaved in wracking breaths, her mouth opening and closing though no sound came out—no sound but those harsh gasps. It looked like she might faint, and Caroline almost left her post to run to her mother's aid.

But Quentin got there instead, catching Heather by the hands and helping her to sit back down. He crouched down in front of her, on one knee, and continued to hold her hands long after he should have let go. A sight that Caroline did not like one bit—no matter how friendly Quentin had been with her father in the past, that did not give the man any right to touch Heather in any capacity. Caroline did not know why it felt so wrong, but every instinct inside her screamed that Quentin's was not a gesture of support. There was something else afoot; she just could not pinpoint what it was.

"*I* will take care of you and your daughters," Quentin said softly, urgently, his gaze fixed upon Heather's face. "*That* is the very least that I can do for my dear friend. Your unborn child, too. You will not have to work, you will not have to worry; you will be safe with me. I swear it. You have known me many years, Heather—you know that I am capable."

Caroline flinched as if she had been struck, hearing him call her mother by her given name, hearing him speak so informally and... intimately to her. Of course, Caroline knew that friends of her father's would, by proxy, have been acquainted with her mother, but she could not think of any of her father's friends who would address Heather like that.

"But... how?" Heather choked. "I couldn't be a burden to you, Quentin. I couldn't."

Quentin... Caroline shuddered again, hating that familiarity.

"You would be no burden to me, Heather," Quentin purred, bringing one of Heather's hands to his lips, kissing it softly. "As soon as it is appropriate, I will marry you. You will be my wife and, as my wife, you will always be safe. I shall make certain of it. You and your family. I owe Adam that much."

A roiling nausea caught Caroline in the stomach,

sending acid bile up her throat as she recoiled from the crack in the wall. It was too vile and too perverse. What sort of wretched beast would ask for a widow's hand in marriage, not two weeks after her husband had died—indeed, before her husband was even in the ground?

Refuse him, Mama. Send him out of this house at once, Mama. Don't stand for it! Caroline urged, too frozen with horror to make any protest of her own. Luke's warning still echoed in her mind; she could not afford to be discovered in her hiding place.

To Caroline's relief, her mother wrenched her hands out of Quentin's, her expression of horror a reflection of the disgust in Caroline's stomach.

"I won't marry again," Heather rasped, shaking her head. "I can't do it. I loved him with all my heart, Mr. Rawle. There is no room for another husband after him. If I must struggle, then so be it. If I must find work, if I must lose these apartments, if I must return to the old days, then—"

As if expecting some resistance, Quentin withdrew a bottle from the pocket of his greatcoat. A brown bottle, so familiar to Caroline that she would have known it by touch alone.

Heather fell silent, her eyes widening, her expression hungry. "You... brought my medicine?"

"Of course, my dear," Quentin replied. "I assumed you would be nearly done with your last bottle, so I took the liberty of purchasing another. I thought you might need it, and I could not abide the thought of you suffering. That is the only reason I am asking you to marry me, when enough time has passed—so you do not suffer."

Heather could not take her eyes off the medicine. "May I?"

"Allow me," Quentin insisted, removing the stopper and pouring a measure into a spoon that he had, suspiciously, brought with him.

Blinking with dreadful realisation, Caroline could not see a second spoon. Before she could even properly register the mistake, Quentin had fed an entire spoonful of the substance to her mother, and her mother had swallowed it greedily, licking her lips, licking the spoon, closing her eyes in deep satisfaction as she savoured the dose.

Sitting back against the cushions of the settee, Heather smiled that dazed smile that Caroline had come to hate. And when her mother's eyes opened, they were as glassy as a doll's.

"You are kind to me, Quentin," she sighed, reaching out to touch his shoulder. "You have always been so kind to me."

Quentin covered her hand with his. "All I want is to continue being kind. So, dear Heather, please say that you will be my wife. Let me take care of you."

"Why not," Heather murmured, chuckling.

Panicking, Caroline grabbed the tea tray she had been preparing and tipped it off the kitchen counter, flinching as it fell to the floor. The cups smashed and the spoons clattered, as she put her eye to the crack in the wall once more. Quentin seemed unbothered by the noise, and Heather had not noticed it.

"I need you to say that you accept my proposal," he urged, as if he knew he might be interrupted at any moment. Worse, as if he knew he was being overheard.

Heather nodded dozily. "I will... be your wife. You will take care of... me. I will never have to... worry."

"No, my dear, you will never have to worry again." Quentin took hold of Heather's hand and brought it to his lips, kissing it gently as Heather sank further back into the settee, her eyelids fluttering shut.

A moment later, the wretched man turned his sharp gaze towards the wall, his two steely grey eyes meeting the one wide, horrified eye that watched him through the crack. Caroline recoiled, heart racing, fear beetling down her spine as she heard Luke's voice repeating in her head: *Mr. Rawle doesn't like anyone knowing his business...*

Breathing hard, Caroline crouched down and began to gather up the shards of teacup with shaky hands, wincing as a sharp edge caught her finger. She put the finger in her mouth, tasting blood, as she hurried to clear away everything else.

She froze at the sound of footsteps in the hallway beyond the kitchen door, staring at the handle like a startled rabbit, willing it not to turn.

But turn it did, a tall, imposing figure blotting out the light from the hall as the door swung open.

"Miss Calder," Quentin said pleasantly, his voice too soft, too sweet. "I was just wondering where the tea things were. Goodness, are you well? What happened?"

Caroline swallowed past the lump of terror in her throat. "I knocked the tray. I won't be long."

"You have cut yourself." Quentin took a step forward. "Here, let me help you."

She stood up and shuffled backwards, putting her body between him and the gap in the wall. "It's quite all right, Mr. Rawle. It's just a scratch, really. Please, return to the parlour—I'll be along shortly with the tea."

"No need." Quentin eyed her, something simmering beneath the surface of his falsely placed gaze. "Your poor mother has fallen asleep, so I shall be taking my leave now."

Caroline nodded. "Very good, Mr. Rawle."

"You ought to be more careful," he warned with a smile. "You might truly hurt yourself if you do not take care. I hope you are not always so clumsy?"

She shook her head. "An accident, Mr. Rawle."

"Of course." His tight smile did not reach his lupine eyes. "Well then, I shall be on my way. Look after your mother in my absence; it appears no one is tending to her properly, and I cannot bear the thought of her being neglected. I shall return in due course, and I expect her to be in a better condition than I found her when I do. Am I understood?"

Caroline clenched her hands into fists, the motion not unnoticed by Quentin's keen eyes, but even if she had possessed the strength to fight him, he would have overwhelmed her easily. She had been trained and educated from her earliest years to be a delicate lady of society; she had never been taught how to throw a punch or kick a man hard enough in the shins that she could cause some damage.

I will learn... she vowed, schooling her expression into something like courtesy.

"Yes, Mr. Rawle," she managed to say, her throat tight with hatred for the man.

He seemed pleased, dropping his chin in a small nod. "Excellent. I look forward to my next visit." He smirked. "Perhaps, I shall actually get some tea next time."

He turned at that, striding down the hallway as if he owned it, letting himself out of the front door as if he was already part of the family, whistling to himself as he went.

Only when the door clicked back into the jamb did Caroline sag back into the counter, hanging her head and sucking in deep breaths as a wave of nausea swept through her. Whether or not her mother had been truly conscious of what she was saying when she had accepted the proposal, it did not matter; Quentin would ensure that he had Heather as his bride, taking the Calder family for himself.

But why? Caroline had no answers for that. All she knew was that something awful had been set in motion, and she was helpless to prevent it. Like faded strokes of charcoal on paper, Heather's medicine had made her forget her husband entirely.

CHAPTER 9

In a small, gloomy chapel, on a rainy February morning, with seagulls shrieking outside the soot-stained windows, Caroline stood with her hands balled and her jaw clenched as she witnessed the greatest crime she had ever beheld in her four-and-ten years.

"We should say something," Esther whispered, smearing tears from her eyes. "We *have* to say something."

Caroline shook her head slowly. "There is nothing *to* say. Mama was very clear—we are not to protest or complain." She took a tremulous breath. "We are to behave... and accept what is happening."

"But... but how *could* she?" Esther rasped, evidently struggling to keep her voice low enough to avoid disturbing the priest and the ceremony.

The girls had been placed at the back of the chapel, instructed to stay quiet and obedient throughout the farce. Caroline did not know how Quentin had done it, but he had wormed his way into their mother's mind, convincing her that he was her saviour and that this would all be for the best. With every spoon of 'medicine,' Heather obeyed and heeded his wishes more and more, to the point where she would not accept any mention of marrying Quentin being a colossal mistake.

Caroline had tried her best to get her mother to see sense, but Quentin had visited more and more over the past few weeks, always undoing any progress that Caroline had made in restoring Heather to the mother she knew and loved. Now, it was too late; Quentin was getting what he wanted, and he would not allow anyone to stop him.

"She is not herself," Caroline murmured, clinging to that rationale with everything she possessed. She would never believe that there was any actual affection between her mother and Quentin, or that her mother would have chosen this if not for the power of the medicine. She could not.

"Is that not more reason to say something?" Esther urged.

Caroline expelled a frustrated sigh. "At this juncture, with mother as she is, she wouldn't be able to listen. There's nothing we can do, other than hope that Mr. Rawle keeps his promises to her—that he is kind, that he takes care of her, that he never lets her worry about anything again."

"And what of us?"

Caroline had no answer to that, though she had suspicions. She had overheard mentions of Cheltenham Ladies' College—a boarding school for girls that had recently been founded, where they would be far enough away from their mother and Quentin to be suitably forgotten. As for the unborn child, she did not dare to think what might happen. A third daughter would be safest, perhaps, for what man wanted to raise another man's son? But it remained to be seen.

"I don't know," Caroline replied, her gaze drifting to the front of the chapel.

One solitary figure sat on Quentin's side of the pews, shoulders hunched, and head bowed, clearly as unimpressed by the occasion as Caroline was. It had been a fair while since she had last seen Luke, and he showed no indication that he wished to acknowledge her.

He had said nothing to anyone upon entering the chapel, Quentin ushering him quickly to the front, and the boy had not turned around once.

I suppose we'll all have to get used to him, too. Caroline frowned, realising just how much their lives were going to change. They would soon move out of the Saint Pancras apartments and into Quentin's townhouse, leaving everything good and familiar behind.

In truth, she had assumed that Luke had been returned to his mother—Quentin's sister—as he had not visited with his uncle at all throughout the past few weeks. Yet, there he was: not as opinionated or confident or rude as he had been before, but very much still in his uncle's custody.

"I shall never forgive her for this," Esther muttered, drawing out her handkerchief to dab at her eyes.

"Don't blame her," Caroline pleaded softly. "She doesn't know what she's doing, and when she realises it, when she doesn't have to take her medicine anymore, it will hit her harder than you can imagine."

Esther sniffed. "Good. I hope she realises what a terrible mistake she has made."

"You don't mean that."

"I assure you; I do."

Caroline sighed, for she had also been struggling with the same conflict. She kept hoping that her mother would snap out of her stupor, that she would see reason before it was too late, and every time Heather had insisted that it was for the best and she was fully aware of the choice she had made, Caroline had fought against the urge to hate her mother.

I will not believe that you have done this consciously. I will not believe that it is not the medicine, corrupting you. Divorce was not a real option, but when Heather finally woke up to what she had done, Caroline was determined to be at her mother's side, to help her run from it if that was what she wanted.

"Quentin Peter Rawle, do you take this woman to be your lawfully wedded wife?" the priest asked, the words setting Caroline's teeth on edge.

At that moment, Luke stood up abruptly, as if he meant to say something to stop the ceremony from continuing. The priest raised an eyebrow at the boy whilst Quentin turned and shot a fearsome look at his nephew; the kind of glare that would strike terror into the heart of even the most courageous warrior.

"Did you want to say something?" the priest asked curtly.

Shaking with the effort of holding his stiff posture, a strange sound bubbled out of Luke—half-cough, half-growl. As he looked at Quentin, the older man's glare darkened, a vicious warning etched across Quentin's face.

"Boy?" the priest prompted. "Do you have something to say?"

Caroline frowned at the interruption, curiosity swelling in her chest and crackling through her veins, urging Luke to speak. If he could stop this wedding, she would forgive everything she had ever thought about him.

"No," Luke snarled. "I have nothing to say."

He slipped out of the pew and marched up the aisle,

Quentin glowering at his back with every step. Luke strode on, and when he got to the back of the chapel where the two girls had been relegated, he paused.

His mouth moved as if trying to get some words out, but it appeared that they would not come. Instead, his eyes softened, creasing at the corners with a pained sadness, his head shaking slightly. A silent apology, though Caroline did not know what he was sorry for. That he could not stop the wedding? That he was as powerless to prevent it as the girls were? That it had come to this at all?

Meeting Caroline's confused gaze for a fleeting moment, he quickly looked away and pressed on, leaving the chapel altogether.

"Continue," Quentin barked at the priest, who jumped at the sudden volume.

"Of course, Mr. Rawle." The priest took a steadying breath... and carried on, sealing Heather's fate before the eyes of God. Heather, who could barely stand on her own, swaying on her feet, her eyes so glazed and glassy that Caroline reasoned she had swallowed a hefty dose of her medicine that morning. Rather, that Quentin had ensured she had a hefty dose, so she could not come to her senses in time.

Even as Heather slurred through her own vows, the priest took no notice, and all too soon, it was done: Mrs. Calder was Mrs. Calder no more, staggering out of the chapel on Quentin's arm as Mrs. Rawle instead.

"I shall never forgive her for this," Esther repeated, as Caroline pulled gently on her arm, leading her out into the grey morning light to face the unknown of their new lives.

"Hurry yourselves!" Quentin barked, as he all but shoved Heather into the waiting carriage.

Caroline ushered Esther along and helped her into the

carriage, for what else could she do? They could not abandon their mother. Indeed, Caroline suspected that was exactly what Quentin wanted, and the last thing she planned to do was give him everything he desired on a silver platter. She would not let that awful man forget whose daughters they were, even if he sent them away.

Settling onto the squabs, Caroline realised that someone was missing. "Is your nephew not joining us, Mr. Rawle?"

Quentin scowled at her. "That boy is going back to his mother as of today." He took a breath, putting on a false smile. "And please, do not refer to me so formally. From now on, you will call me 'Father.'"

"Oh, Mr. Rawle, I couldn't possibly do that," Caroline replied, wondering where on earth Luke had gone... and if there was room there for two more runaways. Three more, if she could just wean her mother off her medicine.

Quentin sniffed. "As you prefer." He paused, a glint of something nasty in his eyes. "But I *would* urge you both to make this easier for yourselves. Right now, I am a friend to you. I should hate to see that change."

As the carriage trundled away from the chapel, Esther clung tighter to Caroline's arm, peering up with fearful eyes as she whispered, "I'm scared, Caro."

Caroline hugged her sister close, for there were no words in the world that could offer comfort now. Quentin had made his stance clear; the girls would obey, or they would pay a steep price. And Caroline did not want either of them to find out what that cost might be.

CHAPTER 10

One Year Later...

"Why is that child screaming?" Quentin hissed, appearing in the doorway of the small bedchamber that had become Caroline and Esther's prison.

There were at least two empty guest bedchambers on the same floor, and servants' quarters up in the attic that would have served the girls well, but Quentin would not allow his stepdaughters the luxury of space, or of feeling like they were remotely welcome. Rather, they were the equivalent of free labour, acting as maids and cooks with the reward of not being taken to the workhouse.

"She cries, Mr. Rawle," Caroline replied tartly. "She's a baby."

She shifted the baby onto her other hip and made soothing sounds, but the child continued to wail. A thin, sickly little girl; Quentin had done everything within his power, short of starving the baby outright, to try and rid himself of one additional problem. But the baby was as strong as her lungs, and they were mighty.

"She does not *stop!*" Quentin snapped back. "It is *your*

duty to get her to stop. I have warned you time and time again of what will happen if you do not do as you are instructed. Do you want your sister to be taken to the orphanage? I can see to it right now if that is your will. Come, hand her over."

Caroline held her baby sister closer, twisting her body away from her vile stepfather, no longer shy about openly glaring at him. She despised the man and did not care if he knew it, though she *did* care about protecting her sisters. Someone had to, and it was not going to be their mother.

Heather had not even named the child. Quentin had not wanted her to, claiming there was "no purpose in it, considering the child will not survive." But that child was six months old now, and still surviving. 'Lambkin,' as Caroline and Esther called her.

"If you would let us go outside," Caroline replied, "if you would let us go upstairs, even, then you would not be able to hear her crying."

Quentin scoffed. "You would run away, you ungrateful little wretches, and I would be left to console your poor mother. I shan't make her suffer any more than she already has because of you, but I *will* demand obedience. Make that creature shut up or I really will take her away, and you will wish you had done as you were asked."

As if Mama would even notice. Caroline held her tongue, bouncing the baby gently on her lap, wishing silently that the child would be quiet for a while.

"I have very important guests arriving at any moment," Quentin continued. "You are not to be seen or heard until the morning. Failure to comply with my wishes will not end well for any of you. Am I understood?"

The urge to launch something at Quentin's head prickled through Caroline's limbs, but she suppressed it swiftly. Had she been alone with no one to take care of, she would have thrown herself at the wretch and pummelled him until he was black and blue, scratched to ribbons, but any misstep that she made would result in punishment for Esther and Lambkin too.

She had learned that the hard way.

"Of course," she said tightly. "We won't dare to make a peep."

Quentin sniffed. "Good. This is an important night for your mother. Do not make her regret having you as her daughters, any more than she already does."

He stormed out, slamming the door behind him—which, of course, launched Lambkin into a fresh bout of deafening screams.

"What is wrong with her, Caro?" Esther asked, crawling out from beneath the narrow, iron-wrought bed that all three daughters shared. She always hid now, whenever she heard footsteps on the stairs.

Caroline smiled wearily at her sister. "There's nothing wrong with her, Estie. She's a baby who has been torn away from her mother, that's all. She is letting everyone know how much she disapproves." She kissed the baby's warm brow. "Goodness, how I wish I could scream at Quentin as loudly."

"But he's right—she doesn't stop crying," Esther murmured, climbing up onto the bed, tucking herself up against the metal headboard, her knees to her chest.

Caroline rocked Lambkin slowly, staring down at the plump red cheeks, the scrunched face, the balled-up fists. If she did not know any better, she would have guessed that her baby sister was in some manner of pain. But a physician *had* assessed her a couple of months ago and had found nothing amiss.

"Just fussy," he had said.

Quentin had taken one of Caroline's bracelets in order to pay for the visit, to make a point that they could not expect any care from him. He had plenty of money of his own, but when it came to any of the girls, he was a wretched miser. For Heather, on the other hand, he could not spend his money quickly enough, transforming her into his little doll, dressing her and primping her until she was the ideal wife. The constant doses of her 'medicine' helped, keeping her malleable and obedient to his every whim.

"She has been that way since she was born," Esther said, frowning at the baby. "I don't remember myself, but I doubt I was like that when I was a baby."

Caroline shrugged. "You were in a household where you were loved. Maybe, Lambkin feels more of the situation than we think. I wouldn't be too happy if I ended up somewhere like this, either." She paused, fixing Esther with a stern look. "But we can't let Quentin take her to an orphanage. As frustrating as it is sometimes, we're all she has, and we have to keep her safe."

Esther nodded, fidgeting with the frayed hem of her dress. "I just don't want to get in trouble again."

"I know." Caroline shuffled over to the small window and held the baby up to the pane, the shivering wails subsiding as Lambkin's big eyes surveyed the world outside their townhouse prison.

The baby pressed her sticky palms to the glass, knees bending in a funny sort of stationary hop, as something like a laugh bubbled out of her throat.

"I'd like to go outside too," Caroline said with a tired smile, her thin arm aching as she continued to hold Lambkin up to the pane.

"Do you know it's your birthday today?" Esther asked.

A breath hitched in Caroline's throat, her sister's words winding her for a second. "I do."

"Do you think Mother remembers?"

Caroline watched a terrier trotting beside its owner, and a handsome couple wander by arm in arm, the gentleman smiling adoringly at the young lady. She watched dead leaves spiral in the breeze and the sway of bare branches in the private park opposite—a beautiful oval of greenery that none of the girls had been allowed to explore.

"I don't know," she admitted. "I don't think she remembers much of anything, these days."

Esther wiped her nose on the back of her sleeve. "We need to take that medicine off her. She was supposed to stop taking it after Lambkin arrived, but she didn't. It's... doing something to her. It has already *done* something to her." Her voice caught in her throat. "The Mama we knew would never allow Quentin to treat us like this. *She* should be caring for Lambkin, not you. *We* should be back in our home, going to school, selling Papa's paintings and keeping his memory alive."

Caroline refused to look at Esther, fearful that the younger girl would see the tears that threatened to well. "It can't be changed, Estie." She hesitated. "I tried to take her bottles of medicine—you know that—but Quentin just bought more, and struck us for stealing. He'll do the same or worse if we try again."

The two sisters fell into an unsettled silence, peppered only by the gurgles and whines of Lambkin, as she decided whether or not to start screaming again. They were all trapped, whether they liked it or not, and no amount of defiance would alter that. If it could, they would have been free by now.

"When the guests arrive for the party, we should sneak upstairs," Esther said suddenly. "It isn't fair that your birthday should pass by like any other day. There are things up there that we can use for a celebration of our own."

Caroline glanced warily at her sister. "We shouldn't do anything that will see us punished."

"That oaf won't notice," Esther insisted.

"I thought you just said you didn't want to get into trouble again."

"I don't, but... I think a morsel of courage is in order, to celebrate this day," Esther said shyly. "You did the same for me on my birthday. And... I think it's what Papa would want me to do."

Caroline smiled at the memory of Esther's birthday. Their mother and Quentin had gone to the theatre, leaving Caroline with the perfect opportunity to create a small party for her sister. She had taken a few things from the kitchen that would not be noticed as missing, had baked a little cake, and used a hairpin to unlock the doors to the garden. It had been summer then, the evening balmy and rich with the scent of sun-warmed flowers, and they had sat out on the terrace and enjoyed their stolen delicacies until the long summer day finally tipped into night. Lambkin had been no more than a couple of weeks old, and had decided to give the older girls some relief that night, sleeping soundly through the modest festivities.

"We'll have to be careful," Caroline said, her heart a little lighter.

Esther mustered a grin. "As you said yourself—we shan't make a peep."

* * *

BUNDLED up in cloaks and blankets, pilfered from the airing cupboard halfway down the narrow corridor of the unused servants' quarters, Caroline and Esther tiptoed the rest of the way to the slanted window at the farthest end. A rudimentary balcony lay just beyond it, a narrow stone ledge providing a place to stand to draw in some fresh air.

Esther had a basket in the crook of her arm, filled with a heel of stale bread that Caroline had kept back from dinner, and a single jar of blackberry preserve that they had found in a different cupboard. There was also a bottle of cloudy lemonade that had seen better days, the colour slightly suspect, but it smelled all right to Caroline.

"I'm sorry I didn't think to make you a cake," Esther said, as they made it to the slanted window.

Caroline checked on Lambkin, who had finally fallen asleep against her chest, wrapped in a sling. "Nonsense. I don't much like cake anyway."

"Fibber."

Caroline chuckled. "The exact thing I want is blackberry jam on bread."

"Double fibber." Esther grinned, resembling the carefree, lively girl she had been just a year ago, before their lives had changed irrevocably. It was rare to see glimpses of that girl, and Caroline savoured the moment, praying it would last a while.

Stealthily, Caroline pushed up the bottom of the sash window, wincing at every scrape and screech of the old mechanism. When the first blast of fresh, cold air struck her, however, she inhaled it in deep gulps as if she had not taken a proper breath in months. It was a medicine greater than anything that could be poured into a bottle, cheering her weary heart as she let the wind sweep in, smiling as it caressed her face.

"I'll go first," Caroline said, ducking through the open window to the balcony beyond.

There, she stamped lightly on the stone lip between the glass and the balcony, making sure it would hold. Satisfied that it was secure, she sat down and let her legs dangle through the bars, shifting to the side to leave room for Esther.

"It's strange," Esther said, sitting down beside her sister. "I used to hate having to leave our home for anything. I was never happier than being curled up in the window seat with one of my books. I didn't think I would ever miss feeling cold air on my face."

Caroline laughed softly. "Papa used to call you a recluse."

"I thought going outside was punishment," Esther agreed, chuckling. "Now, I'd give anything to walk to school with Papa one more time. Even if it was pouring rain, I'd go without complaint if I could just walk with him again."

"Me too."

Esther glanced up at her sister. "Do you think Mama will remember the anniversary? It's... coming soon."

"I think part of her will remember," Caroline replied after a moment, her heart sore at the realisation that it was almost a year since they lost their father—the best man she had ever known.

A year since Caroline had held him in her arms as he took his last breath. A year since they had wandered along the snowy streets in the midst of a blizzard, singing 'All Things Bright and Beautiful' to each other, making up the words, filling the air with their discordant voices as they joined in with the chorus. A year since she had last felt true happiness. A year since the worst day of her life.

"I miss him," Esther mumbled.

"Me too." Caroline rested her brow on the balcony bars, gazing out at the wintry evening, and the uniform townhouses of Mayfair.

She looked towards the warm, welcoming lights of neighbours, trying to imagine the lives that were unfurling within those houses. She imagined girls her age, worrying over tea parties, quarrelling with friends, and fretting over what manner of man they might marry in a few years—things that Caroline used to worry about in a different life.

Guilt pricked inside her stomach as she drew her gaze across the rooftops, to the parts of London that she could not see. True, her life had become more difficult, existing as prisoners in the house of a man who hated the three daughters, but there were worse situations to be in. All across the city, there were people who did not know when they might eat again, people who had no roof over their heads, people who had to huddle into doorways on a freezing night like this, uncertain if they would survive until morning.

To them, we are lucky. I shouldn't forget that.

"When I marry," Caroline said, "I will bring you and Lambkin with me."

Esther leaned into her sister. "Do you promise?"

"I do. In a few years, we'll get out of here," Caroline replied. "I'll marry the first gentleman who seems pleasant enough, who will accept the two of you as well as me."

"What if such a man turns out to be exactly like Quentin?" Esther asked.

"Then, I'll take whatever I can, and we'll run until we are somewhere that we will not be found," Caroline assured, meaning every word. "All we have to do until then is stay together."

Esther weaved her arm through her sister's. "And what about Mama?"

"We can come back for her," Caroline said. "We can kidnap her, take away her medicine, and hope that she can be restored to who she was before that wretched beast came along."

Esther sighed. "I like the sound of that." She hesitated. "Do you ever wonder what happened to that boy?"

"Which boy?"

"Quentin's nephew." Esther peered up at her. "I always hoped he might visit, so I could ask what he was going to say at the wedding."

Caroline had thought about Luke fairly often over the past year, wishing the same thing. She was certain that Luke had been about to say something compelling that day, and it had driven her to distraction that she had never been able to find out what.

But, since that day, it was as if Luke had never existed. Whenever Caroline had mentioned him to Quentin, Quentin had acted as if both girls were quite mad, insisting that he did not know who they were talking about. If it were not for Esther, agreeing that Luke was real, Caroline would have been convinced that she had imagined him.

"I think Quentin got rid of a problem, as he might do with us if we aren't cautious," Caroline replied, thinking her most unsettling thoughts aloud.

Esther shuddered, nestling closer to her sister.

As they sat there in silence, not touching the bread and blackberry jam they had brought to share, the sounds of the party below began to drift up to their rooftop perch. Soft music and chatter, the clink of glasses, the explosive laughter of someone who had already imbibed a great deal.

Caroline closed her eyes and imagined her mother down there, clinging to Quentin's arm, dressed in a fine gown that he had chosen for her. She pictured her mother wearing rouge on her cheeks, her lips painted, her beautiful auburn hair fashioned into a complicated style, barely able to stand upright after her latest dose of medicine. A delicate creature to be admired and observed, who did not need to be able to speak or stand alone—that was not the purpose she served as Quentin's wife. She had become little more than an adornment for him.

The Mama I know would be appalled by herself. Caroline opened her eyes, wishing—not for the first time—that her mother would wake up and take her girls away from all of this.

But Caroline no longer believed that wishes came true. She could have sipped the Sadler's Well dry, and it would not have made a jot of difference.

CHAPTER 11

Caroline stirred to Lambkin fussing, the sky still dark outside the dirty window of their shared bedchamber. She rubbed her tired eyes and pulled the baby closer, hoping that Lambkin would settle until the sun came up at least. But the baby continued to fuss and whimper, forcing Caroline to sit up and reach for the ceramic jar that contained Lambkin's milk.

"Is this what you want?" Caroline yawned, bringing the spout to Lambkin's mouth, tipping gently so the baby would not choke on the liquid.

Lambkin drank the milk down contentedly, for though she had begun to eat some solid foods, she really *would* have starved if Caroline had relied solely upon that. Something she had been forced to explain to Quentin, when he had asked why he was still paying for the milk.

"It should be eating like a proper person by now," he had tried to protest.

"She will die if she doesn't keep having her milk. Weaning takes a while. It will be several months more before she can have just food, as we know it," Caroline had replied, having read

several books on motherhood that Quentin had given to her. Without doubt, he had meant the books to be some sort of insult or sardonic offering, not realising that they had actually proven to be very useful. Instrumental, in fact, in keeping Lambkin alive.

Stifling a jaw-aching yawn, Caroline paused, pricking her ears. An unusual noise thudded its way into the tiny bedchamber where Esther, at least, still lay sound asleep.

Footsteps.

Who would be awake at such an hour? Caroline frowned at the bedchamber door, hoping beyond all hope that it might be her mother. It was rare, after one of Quentin's raucous parties, for anyone to be awake before noon. Many guests stayed at the townhouse until they had been relieved of the worst of their post-inebriation regret and sickness, which ordinarily meant that Caroline and her sisters were to remain in that room until the last had gone.

Has a guest lost their way? She held her breath, hardly daring to move. Quentin would be furious if any of his acquaintances discovered that he had three secret step-daughters, hidden away in the equivalent of a storage room, in a corner of the house that no one had any reason to visit.

The door handle turned, and Caroline considered lying back down to pretend to sleep, but with the milk jar in her hand and the baby in her arms, it could not be done.

She blinked in uneasy bewilderment as the door opened to reveal Quentin, looking rather fresh-faced and dressed in a fine suit with his greatcoat already on, his top hat perched upon his head.

"Good. You are awake." Quentin smiled. "Rouse the other one, get dressed, and put on your coats. We are going on a little excursion."

Caroline narrowed her eyes at her stepfather. "Where to?"

"Your mother is in great distress," Quentin replied, an annoyed edge to his voice. "As such, I am taking you and your sisters on a brief trip to stay with my parents in Leeds."

Leeds? She knew of the city but had never ventured further north than St. Alban's, when her father had taken her to visit a portrait client. As far as she was aware, Leeds was all the way up the country, in the county of Yorkshire. Not the sort of place that anyone would go to for a 'brief' visit.

Caroline remembered to tip the bottle, listening to the happy sounds of Lambkin feeding. "How long do you expect we will be there?"

"I will not lie to you, Caroline," he replied tightly, "you will be in the care of my parents for a few weeks—a month at most. But they are good people; they will look after you, and you might even find that you prefer it to being here."

No, you mean you *will prefer it if we aren't nearby anymore.* She was not stupid; she knew exactly what he was doing, but she did *not* know what had caused him to make this decision. Had Heather come to her senses last night? Had she remembered it was her eldest daughter's birthday? Had she remembered that her beloved husband had died almost a year ago? It seemed likely, if Caroline's mother was suddenly 'in distress.' And Quentin did not like when his doll remembered.

"I don't trust you," she said bluntly.

"Your mother needs time to rest and recuperate," Quentin insisted. "It will be for a month at most."

Caroline held his cold gaze. "I must repeat—I don't trust you." She took a breath. "If you don't send for us in a month, if you don't make arrangements for our return, rest assured that I will find a way for us to come back. You won't be rid of us that easily. Indeed, as long as my mother draws breath, we shall always be nearby."

He shrugged. "Believe what you will, but I intend for you to return. If I did not bring you back, your mother would only be in greater distress. Unbearable distress, in truth." He huffed out an irritated sigh. "She is aware of this sojourn and believes it will also be for the best. But it will not be worth the complaints if I do not return you to this house in a month's time, at the latest. Trust in that if you will not trust in me. I do not like inconvenience. Your absence would be extremely inconvenient for me and my wife."

Caroline eyed him warily, uncertain what to make of his words. She was not in the habit of believing anything that came out of his mouth, but his demeanour was not what she was accustomed to. There was no smirking, no sly look in his eyes, no subterfuge that she could detect. Rather, he seemed like a man at the end of his tether, who was none-too-pleased with the turn of events.

"Do your parents know about us?" Caroline asked.

Quentin sniffed. "They do. They have been hoping to meet you all, but *I* have delayed it. Now, everyone gets what they want, aside from my coffers—I shall have to employ a maid and a cook for these irksome weeks."

"Who will take care of my mother whilst you take us to Leeds?" Caroline would not relent so easily, though she had to wonder if a month away, in a new place where they might be permitted some freedom would not be a welcome thing indeed.

He clenched his jaw. "Friends of mine have agreed to stay with her until I return. Mr. and Mrs. Shenton. They are, at present, in the guest chamber down the hallway." Visibly more vexed, he gestured to the window. "Now, hurry up. The carriage will leave in half an hour, whether you are all ready or not."

He closed the door behind him, his footsteps retreating down the hallway, the creak and groan of the staircase letting Caroline know that he would be waiting for them. If they did not comply, she wondered if he would come back and drag them downstairs, one by one.

"I think we should go," a soft voice whispered from beneath a mountain of coverlets. "Maybe, if we're not here, Mama will remember us more."

A pale face emerged from beneath the coverlets; Esther's hair sticking up at all angles, her eyes more hopeful than Caroline had seen them in a year.

"And when we come back," Esther continued nervously, "maybe she'll be better. Maybe she'll care about us again."

Caroline chewed her lip in thought, torn between bolstering her sister's hope and not trusting Quentin. Then again, she had made her promise to Quentin: if he did not arrange for their return, she would see to it that they made their way back to their mother. She had meant that with every fibre of her being. As such, there could be no real harm in seeing if they could find some fleeting peace and happiness in Yorkshire.

Mama will still be here. And perhaps Esther is right— absence might just make the heart grow fonder. Make it remember, at the very least.

"I'll gather Lambkin's things," Caroline said, praying she was not making a mistake. "You dress yourself and pack a few belongings. We don't have long."

"This will be good for us," Esther insisted, in a voice far

more mature than her years. A phrase she had clearly picked up somewhere.

Caroline nodded. "I hope so, Estie, for all our sakes." She paused. "Might you watch Lambkin for a few minutes. I just need to do something before we leave."

"What?" Esther asked, raising an eyebrow.

"Give Mama something to ensure that she uses this time to remember who she was, and who she ought to be thinking about. Something to make sure she doesn't forget us," Caroline replied, passing the baby into Esther's outstretched arms, before reaching for something underneath the pillows.

Holding the retrieved item against her chest, Caroline tiptoed barefoot across the small room and let herself out into the hallway, pausing to listen for any movement. Hearing nothing, she crept along as quietly as possible, halting again at the landing.

She peered around the wall that bordered the staircase and squinted through the gloom to the entrance hall. Quentin was not there. Most likely, he had gone to fetch some breakfast for himself before the long journey.

Seizing her opportunity, Caroline darted across the landing and into the opposite hallway, not stopping until she reached the door of her mother's chambers. Already certain that Quentin would not be inside, for she had heard him make his way downstairs, she opened the door and slipped inside without hesitation.

Inside the darkened room, illuminated only by the fire that flickered in the grate to stave off the winter cold, Caroline looked towards the bed. Her heart cracked as she saw her mother lying there, curled up on her side, one hand tucked under her cheek, facing her daughter. Heather looked peaceful, breathing softly in her sleep, romantic auburn curls framing her still-beautiful face.

"Mama?" Caroline whispered, approaching.

Heather did not stir, though Caroline had not truly expected her to. After taking her heftier nightly dose of medicine, an entire marching band could not have woken her.

"Mama, remember us," Caroline said, unfurling the piece of paper she had taken from beneath her own pillow.

On it, in perfect detail, were the two girls, seated on the chaise-longue in their father's studio, attempting to draw the objects that he had set out for them. The sketch he had made of them a year ago, his talent and his love for his daughters shining through in every line and smudged shading of the drawing.

"Remember that you're our mama, and we want you back," Caroline added as, with a sad sigh, she folded the sketch back up and slid it beneath her mother's pillow.

Holding back tears, Caroline leaned in and kissed her mother's hot brow, whispering, "We love you, Mama. We'll be back soon," against her smooth skin.

With that, Caroline hurried back out to gather her things and her sisters, hoping with everything she possessed that the situation would be different when they returned.

Remember us. Remember it all, no matter how much it hurts. I beg of you.

CHAPTER 12

Despite all of her doubts, Caroline took some relief in the fact that the carriage *did* appear to be heading north. She made a point to peer out of the window and squint at every passing way-marker, just to be sure, and with each one that the carriage went by, the miles between London and Leeds slowly ticked down.

The day passed with fewer milestones to mark the time inside the carriage's stuffy interior; the dawn light barely brightening into an overcast morning that became greyer by the hour, before rain began to spit against the windows shortly before luncheon. The sparse meal was eaten in the carriage, the rain refusing to relent as the hours bled into afternoon, traipsing sluggishly towards evening.

All the while, Lambkin had screamed and cried in Caroline's arms. Quentin had watched the baby with a vicious scowl upon his face, his ears stuffed with balls of wax, sitting so rigid on the squabs that one fierce jolt of the wheels in a rut would see him fly forwards. Alas, no such ditch had come along to give Caroline *something* to smile about.

"How long do you expect it will take to reach your parents' residence?" Caroline asked, as sunset streaked the muted sky with splinters of burnished orange and blushing pink. Nightfall would be upon them soon, and she did not like the idea of trying to soothe Lambkin through the dark hours, when Esther—and certainly Quentin—would need some sleep.

Quentin turned his gaze out of the window. "Another day or two."

"Pardon?" Caroline's eyes bulged, her heart sinking.

"Did you think it would be a swift journey?" Quentin snorted. "I thought you were supposed to be educated."

"I have never thought to look at where Leeds might be on a map," Caroline retorted as curtly as she dared. "Nor have I had a moment to do the arithmetic, to gauge the time and distance. I have been too busy cleaning your house and cooking your meals."

Quentin's head twisted around, his steely eyes glinting. "That *witty* tongue might get you in trouble one of these days." He stretched his arms, relaxing his shoulders. "Anyway, is that not what daughters are for? You do not see the daughters of Whitechapel or Cheapside or Poplar complaining that they have to scrub a floor or two. You are too spoiled still; that is your trouble."

Lambkin's ear-splitting wails prevented Caroline from making a smart remark, a shudder running through Quentin at the sound. Shifting Lambkin in her arms, cradling her, Caroline did her best to quieten the poor thing, but the baby could not be consoled. Her big eyes scrunched and widened, as if she were in some unimaginable pain, and there was nothing Caroline could do to help. Nothing anyone did would help.

"We will be stopping soon," Quentin muttered. "I hope that beast is quieter then. I do not want it disturbing anyone."

Caroline glared at the man. "She is not a beast, nor is she an 'it'. I pray that your mother and father can see that, even if you can't."

"And I pray that *you* finally learn how to behave yourselves," Quentin shot back, grimacing as he no doubt heard the weakness of the retort.

Still, Caroline would have been lying if she had said she was not looking forward to stopping somewhere. Her legs and sides ached from having to twist herself into uncomfortable positions in an attempt to soothe Lambkin, and her backside had gone completely numb after so many hours sitting on the squabs, jostled by the rattling carriage wheels.

Perhaps we could run, she daydreamed. *I could find work, take care of my sisters, and when we are older, we can return to my mother and steal her away.* It was a lovely thought, but she had a feeling that Quentin had already considered a potential escape. He would not let any of the girls out of his sight.

An hour later, as inky darkness blotted out the colourful sunset and the last of the dusky light receded to make way for shadow, the carriage turned off the main country road.

The girls clung onto whatever they could to avoid being thrown from the squabs as the relative smoothness of the road gave way to a dirt track, riddled with divots and ruts. Quentin swayed and moved with the motions, as if he were seated in the saddle of a particularly wild mount, unbothered by the violent change in terrain.

Lambkin, too, seemed bizarrely comforted by the rocky

journey, her big eyes fluttering closed as Caroline held her tightly.

You are a strange one, Lambkin. But I suppose it is to be expected.

At length, soft lights appeared in the distance: the glow of a village that had not yet retired for the night, guiding the carriage and its passengers to a welcoming sanctuary after such a weary expedition. Caroline could almost feel the pillow underneath her head and the food that she might savour beside a fireplace, surrounded by warmth and chatter to lift her heavy spirits.

"Is this where we're staying for the night?" she asked, trying not to sound too eager.

Quentin shrugged. "It is as good a place as any. Almost halfway between London and Leeds. Quite pleasant."

The carriage continued on down the track, veering left into the stable yard of what appeared to be an inn. A thatched roof adorned the lopsided building, the whitewashed walls interspersed with dark beams of timber, as gauzy light spilled from small windows in the upper floor. From within, the sound of music drifting towards Caroline's ears, and her heart sang with tentative joy, imagining the merry scene inside.

"Wait here," Quentin commanded. "I must see if they have rooms for us."

Caroline's enthusiasm waned a little, certain that it would crush her if there was nowhere for them to stay. Esther was already lolling against the squabs, struggling to keep her eyes open, and Lambkin would sleep better in a warm room with somewhere soft and safe to lie down.

Flashing a warning look at Caroline, Quentin exited the carriage and slid the bolt he had installed, keeping the girls locked inside. With that, he disappeared into the darkness.

"What if he takes a room for himself and doesn't come back?" Esther murmured, rubbing her tired eyes.

"Then we'll make the best of it in here," Caroline replied, hearing the false brightness in her voice and hoping that her sister would not notice.

As they waited for Quentin to return, a cart clattered across the cobbles, coming to a standstill a short distance away.

Peeking out from behind the small curtains of the carriage window, Caroline observed the new arrivals: two burly, thick-set men sat on the driver's bench, one puffing away on a pipe whilst the other stretched out muscular arms. A canvas tarpaulin covered the back of the cart, concealing the men's cargo from prying eyes like Caroline's.

At that moment, a figure emerged from the inn, greatcoat swishing against the cobblestones. Caroline's heart dared to soar as she realised it was Quentin, only to sink again as she watched him walk towards the men on the cart instead of back towards the carriage.

It means nothing, she told herself, struggling to swallow the rising dread that stung its way up her throat, cutting off her ability to breathe.

The men got down and, joining Quentin, they approached the carriage.

"All three of 'em?" one of the men asked, peering through the window as if he were observing curios at the British Museum.

Quentin nodded. "All three of them."

What? Panic wriggled in Caroline's chest, constricting her ribs until she could not catch a lungful of air. All she could do was put her arm around Esther, holding her close, and curve herself around Lambkin as if that could protect them.

"What age?" the second man asked.

"Five-and ten, eleven, and the baby is but half a year," Quentin replied, leaning against the side of the carriage, too cowardly to bother looking at his stepdaughters. "How much? Your associate in London mentioned a price, but I am certain you are haggling men."

The second man took another intent look at the girls. "The littlun will do for the farm. Older lasses might do for the farm an' all. If they can't be of use there, they'll be good enough for the mills." He smirked. "The price for the wain won't change, but we'll take the older lasses for naught. Lasses are always useful somewhere."

Grumbling something under his breath, Quentin took out a weighty pouch of coins and dropped it into the other man's extended hand. "I trust that will be enough for the 'care' of the child for a while."

"If it ain't, Mr. Fox will be sure to let you know," the man replied with a brown-toothed grin.

Quentin stepped away from the carriage. "Take them, then. And quickly. I do not want any trouble."

He slid back the bolt as Caroline's mind caught up to what was happening, realisation hitting her like a kick to the chest. These men were not interested in her and Esther; the older girls were just an additional and unexpected benefit. No, these men were interested in the baby, and the money that Quentin had just paid for them to take Lambkin away.

The littlun will do for the farm...

Nausea seized Caroline's stomach in an iron grip. She had heard about the infamous 'Baby Farms,' but she had always thought they were a myth to scare children, a means to get sons and daughters to do as they were told. She had never in her life suspected that they might be real—the last resort for desperate women who hoped to, one day, return for their child.

But Quentin is not a desperate woman, nor does he want our mother to ever return for her child... He had paid the money to alleviate his own guilt, and by the time it ran out, Caroline knew that Quentin would have forgotten all about his stepdaughters and any guilt he might have felt about what would befall them after.

Either that, or he had judged this to be his best option. After all, if he had placed them in an orphanage, it would have been easier for the girls to escape and come back to tell the tale to their mother of what her husband had done. With money at risk, these terrifying men would make sure the girls did not escape. They were little more than handsomely paid gaolers.

I have to get everyone to safety. Think, Caro, think! Her mind raced as the first man wrenched open the carriage door.

The second man lunged forward without hesitation, grabbing Esther by the wrist, pulling hard. Caroline tried to hold on to her sister, tried to prevent the inevitable, tried to ignore her sister's cries of pain as she was wrenched between the two, but the man was too strong. Caroline's hand slipped and the man dragged Esther out, throwing her to the ground.

In the blink of an eye, he was already lunging back in to drag Caroline and Lambkin out into the cold.

As Caroline stumbled forwards, almost falling on her face, and the man released his grip for half a second, she saw her one and only chance. Clutching Lambkin close, Caroline scraped up a handful of the dusty soil that covered the stable yard and threw it with all her might into the man's eyes. He bellowed and staggered back, rubbing frantically at his face. And as the other man surged forwards, Caroline did the one thing she had never dared to do before, though she had been practicing; she drove her knee upwards with all the force she could muster, catching the man squarely where it would hurt the most.

Quentin looked on in utter shock, and in his delay, Caroline ran for Esther, yanked her up off the ground, and took off out of the stable yard, pulling her sister along with her.

"Run, Estie! You have to run!" Caroline urged as they skidded out of the yard and onto the dirt track that eventually connected to the road.

Esther's legs did their best to keep up, both older girls haring along, driven by the panic that they would be caught if they did not. There were no streetlamps to see by; the moon hidden behind rainclouds, the girls running blind down the track.

"If I'm captured," Caroline wheezed, "you have to keep running. You have to… take Lambkin and… keep running."

She heard footfalls thudding on the earth behind them, her heart threatening to burst with the fear that pummelled through her veins. But she could not stop. Freedom lay ahead of them, imprisonment lay behind them; it was no choice at all.

By the Grace of God, they managed to tear through the gap in the hedgerows that marked the beginning of the dirt track, their sprint to liberty accompanied by the grunts and expletives of the men stumbling and falling somewhere behind them. The darkness was not a curse but an advantage, and it truly felt as if a divine force was guiding the girls as they ran on, turning up the country road.

If they had cut across to the fields opposite or hidden themselves in the coppice of trees nearby or ducked down behind the hedgerows, perhaps they would have escaped. But the road was too open and too well-travelled, the surface smooth, giving the two men the opportunity to catch up to the fleeing girls.

A rough hand seized the back of Caroline's dress, tearing the seam at the neck as she was wrenched backwards. Meanwhile, strong arms wrapped around Esther, hoisting her up. She kicked and screamed and protested, but a hand across her mouth soon silenced that.

"The baby!" Caroline croaked, the wind knocked out of her. "Be careful... of the baby!"

The man glowered down at her, snatching Lambkin straight out of Caroline's arms. "Don't you worry about the wain. You worry about yourself," he snarled, his grip tightening on her wrist as he pulled her along... back to the stable yard.

In the low torchlight that illuminated the rear of the inn, Quentin stood with a smirk on his face.

"Why are you doing this?" Caroline rasped, her lungs on fire.

Quentin strutted towards the cart. "You have to ask?"

"Mama won't let you get away with this," she insisted bitterly. "She'll remember us, and she'll come for us. And when she finds out what you did, she'll have the constables at your door before you can even think to pour her another spoonful of that awful medicine."

Quentin laughed coldly, clearly enjoying himself as Esther's hands were tied and she was thrown into the back of the cart, beneath the tarpaulin. He grinned all the wider as the men came to tie Caroline's hands, binding them in front of her so they could thrust the baby into her arms.

"Your dear mother will be as glad to be rid of you as I am," Quentin replied. "A new beginning for us both, without reminders of her inferior marriage."

"You promised her you would take care of us all," Caroline spat. "I knew you were lying, even then."

Quentin feigned innocence. "Then, you should have said something."

"You fed her so much of that medicine that she wouldn't listen, regardless of what I said."

He shrugged. "Never mind, then." He paused, coming closer, touching his vile fingertips to Caroline's cheek. "Did you honestly think that I would raise another man's ungrateful little urchins? Your father was a fool, but I am not. Now, *you* might have fetched a handsome dowry from an eager suitor, but I shall manage without that."

Lambkin whimpered in Caroline's arms.

Quentin pulled a face. "I shall not be sorry to never hear that thing crying again." He looked to the men. "Take them and be quicker about it."

Muttering obscenities at being told what to do, the two men dragged Caroline towards the rear of the cart and duly threw her into the back, beneath the musty canvas. It was impossible to see anything within that bizarre tent, but Caroline sensed the presence of others—soft breaths, quiet sniffles, the shift and sour scent of uneasy bodies.

Immediately, Lambkin began to wail, as if she knew exactly what awaited her at the end of this journey.

"Hush, sweetling," Caroline murmured, struggling to rock the child with her hands bound. "Please, hush."

"Let me try," a strangely familiar voice offered from the opposite side of the cart. "I'm good with littluns."

Caroline blinked, urging her eyes to adjust to the gloom. As if summoned, the moon crept out from behind the rainclouds, casting silvery light through the tarpaulin, illuminating the boy she had been told she had imagined. A boy she had never thought she would see again.

"Luke?" she whispered.

He smiled tightly. "Seems that way."

CHAPTER 13

An owl hooted somewhere in the distance to mark the lateness of the hour, and the screams of quarrelling foxes sent a shiver up Caroline's spine—the sound so human, like someone in distress, that it conjured terrible visions in her mind.

Esther had fallen asleep a while ago, as well as—by some miracle—the baby. Lambkin lay curled up peacefully in Luke's arms, one tiny hand gripping a fistful of his loose, dirty shirt. He had not been lying when he had said he was good with children, though Caroline had to wonder how he had learned such skills.

"Do you have siblings?" she asked him in a hushed whisper, so as not to wake any of the three other young children who were asleep in the cart. Destined for the mills or the mines, according to Luke.

Luke shook his head. "None that I know of." He smiled down at Lambkin. "I was left with my grandma. She took care of about a million babies in the place we were living, and I helped her up until the day she died."

"I thought you were... Quentin's sister's boy?"

Luke snorted. "Quentin doesn't have a sister."

"Then, how did you end up with him?"

"My grandma told me about him before she died," Luke replied. "Said I was his bastard son. Once I'd buried her, I had no place else to go, so I went to his door and told him who I was. Never thought he'd want to take me in. Suppose I was useful to him for a while, and he liked the idea of having a son. Kept saying he'd make me legitimate, but I ended up disappointing him, so he had me sent away—same as you and your sisters."

Caroline swallowed thickly, her wrists sore where the ropes rubbed. "How did you disappoint him?" She hesitated. "Was it the wedding day?"

He chuckled darkly. "It was."

"I've always wondered what you were going to say," she prompted, hoping he would tell her willingly.

He frowned, pinching his lower lip between his teeth for a moment. "I was going to say that he was a swindler who'd tricked your ma into marrying him. I was going to say that he wasn't worthy of her, and couldn't be trusted after... all he'd done to get her, but... I reckon I didn't say anything for the same reason that neither you nor your sister did either. Your ma wouldn't have listened. Too far gone."

Regret twisted Caroline's stomach into knots, wondering how different things might have been if someone had said something. Maybe, it *would* have changed the course of the future. Maybe, her mother would have listened.

"What do you mean?" she asked quietly.

"That 'medicine' she's been taking," Luke replied, his

brow still furrowed. "Terrible stuff. Laudanum. Half the babies that my grandma took care of were left there because their mothers were ruined by it, unable to do anything but take more and more to escape their lives. It's why this littlun cries so much; I've seen it over and over. I don't know how it happens, but it's like they need the laudanum too, and since they can't get it, they scream. I think it hurts them, somehow."

Caroline gasped, staring at Lambkin with fresh eyes. All this time, she had known that something was amiss with the baby, but to hear that she had been right was no relief.

"There's no cure for the screaming other than time," Luke added reassuringly.

Sitting back against the side board of the cart, Caroline struggled to process everything he was saying. It filled in so many gaps in her mind yet begged more questions.

"It has been a year since I last saw you. How are you only just being taken away?" she said haltingly, feeling her way through her words.

"I'm not. I go where those idiots go." Luke pointed up the cart to where the driver's bench was. "I help with the babies and work at the mills, though we don't usually come so far away from Leeds. I guess Quentin made a hefty offer that Mr. Fox thought was worth the additional miles."

"Mr. Fox?" She had heard one of the men mention that name.

He nodded. "It's who I work for. Who *they* work for. He has textile mills in Leeds, plus a few other enterprises." He flashed her a pointed look. "I'm technically an apprentice at the mill, but I work for no pay, barely any food, and not much of a roof over my head. I expect it'll be the same for you."

"Other enterprises," Caroline murmured, grimacing. "You mean 'baby farms'?"

He shifted on the bench, carefully moving Lambkin into the crook of his other arm. "Mr. Fox prefers to call it an orphanage-for-profit, but yes."

"What happens there?"

He took a breath. "Babies that are born out of wedlock or that are unwanted are taken in for a price. They're raised there, while the 'farm' gets a monthly sum from the mothers or families, until the mothers can take them back. Trouble is, the mothers rarely do. It gets too costly, or their circumstances don't change. And once the money stops coming..."

"What?" Caroline stared at him, already knowing the answer but unwilling to believe it.

Luke went very silent and still. He did not need to put the awful truth into words.

"Tell me, Luke," she urged, needing to hear it.

"For a higher, final sum, the babies can be 'adopted' by the farms. The mothers and families believe the child is safe and has a new family but, really, Mr. Fox just puts them straight into the mills, soon as they're old enough. If no one can pay and they'll be of no use in the mills, the children are... given no care."

Caroline nodded to show she understood what that meant.

"As the adopted ones are technically Mr. Fox's children, he gets free labour at his mills, and no one can argue as they're his to do with as he likes," Luke concluded, putting the hooked knuckle of his forefinger to Lambkin's mouth as she started to stir. She suckled on it, quickly settling again.

Greater, more terrible understanding dawned as she glanced down at Esther, and looked back at Lambkin. The amount of coin that had exchanged hands between Quentin and the men had not been enough for adoption, and certainly was not enough for lasting maintenance.

"When you say the other children are given no care, what do you mean? What do they do to the babies no one can pay for?" She had to ask. She had to know, so she could begin planning how to get her sisters away from such a place.

"Depends how much *you* care for them," Luke replied, his eyes gleaming in the darkness. "There are ways to prevent bad things happening. And... I can help you."

She frowned at him, grateful and suspicious in equal measure. "Why would you do that?"

"Because I feel like I owe you," he replied, his voice strangely tight. "For not saying anything when I could have, I owe you. For not... stopping Quentin, I owe you. I didn't know of his plans, but I should've seen it. I should've guessed what he was up to."

"The medicine?"

He shrugged. "Among other things."

"What other things?" she pressed.

He shook his head. "Just... the things that led to you being here, and your mother being in a laudanum daze back in London."

Caroline had a feeling she was not going to be able to get him to elaborate, but perhaps she did not need him to— she knew well enough what he meant: the daily visits, the manipulation, the false promises, the sly manner in which he had persuaded the girls to leave the townhouse, the price he was willing to pay to have Heather all to himself.

"You should sleep," Luke said. "It's a fair way until we reach Leeds."

She knew she would not be able to, but with so much to

think about, she lay down on the cart bench and closed her eyes. Almost a year on from the day that had changed their lives forever, it seemed their world was about to change again, and certainly for the worse.

CHAPTER 14

Caroline did not know if it was the same day or another day entirely as the cart left the countryside behind and trundled through the cramped and crowded streets of Leeds. Dusky light and the glow of the cart lanterns reflected in the slick pavements and roads, candles and lamps crackling into life in soot-streaked windows, whilst loud and almost foreign voices yelled from doorways and street corners. Thickly accented English, a world away from the Capital.

"Welcome home," Luke said drily, as he fed Lambkin pieces of bread soaked in milk.

All throughout the journey, he had taken responsibility for the baby, reluctant to hand her back as if he found comfort in holding her and taking care of her. In truth, Caroline was grateful for the reprieve, though she would never have admitted it.

"Is this where we'll stay?" Caroline whispered, nerves jittering.

He nodded. "You two and this'un will. The 'farm' always needs lasses to take care of the babies and infants.

Those three," he pointed his chin towards the three young boys who were sound asleep in the back of the cart once more, "they'll continue up to the mines. I reckon I only got 'apprenticed' to the mills because I'm Quentin's bastard, else I'd be breaking my back in the mines too."

Caroline shuddered, staring sadly at the three boys. "Poor mites. Is there nothing we can do?"

"Not for them." He levelled a stern look at her. "From now on, you need to watch out for your own. No one else."

"But—"

"*No one* but your own," he interrupted. "This isn't a world you know, so trust me. If there's one thing I've learned, it's that you can't save everyone. You'll be lucky if you can save everyone closest to you."

Caroline blinked, dropping her chin to her chest as the carriage rattled on through a labyrinth of dingy, noisy streets. She could have been in Whitechapel or Camden Town, were it not for the different voices: the poor, overcrowded parts of the city where her father had never allowed her to walk unaccompanied.

And they appeared to be venturing deeper and deeper into the seediest, most unsettling part of *this* city. The buildings seemed to lean in, the bombardment of voices getting louder, slurred with cheap alcohol, the faces of passing souls becoming more gaunt, more wild-eyed, more desperate.

At last, the cart broke out of the shadows and into a wide square. There might have been grass in the centre once, but it was barren now, an eyesore of rubble and detritus that had been dumped there.

The buildings that surrounded the square had a faded grandeur, their beauty left to rot in this tucked-away corner of the city. Judging by the sheer quantity of clothes that hung from lines that crisscrossed out of windows, and the noise that swept across the square, there were a lot of people crammed into those buildings.

The cart halted outside a building that almost stood alone, devoid of clotheslines and din. An old, dilapidated structure of reddish brown stone, Gothic in style, with a crumbling spire and arched windows where cracks spiderwebbed.

"This is it," Luke said, shuffling out of the back of the cart. "It'll be easier if you don't struggle. Mr. Fox has eyes everywhere. He'd find you in this city before you'd even thought of a hiding place."

A shiver of distrust moved through Caroline's chest, wondering if he was more a part of this than he was letting on—someone who put the captives at ease by pretending to be on their side. Still, as Luke had Lambkin in his arms, Caroline had no choice but to wake Esther and follow.

The moment they were out of the cart, the men on the bench snapped the reins, for they had another delivery to make. Caroline spared a thought for the sleeping boys in the back of the cart, hoping that their fate would not be so awful.

Who am I kidding? She expelled a breath and, hugging Esther close to her side, headed into the Gothic building.

* * *

LUKE GUIDED the way through cavernous hallways, the parquet floor sagging and worn to a shine from years of feet, the icy creep of a harsh draught making Caroline's skin prickle into gooseflesh, piercing through the thick wool of her cloak and winter dress.

"This is Mr. Fox's study," Luke explained, pausing in

front of a set of mahogany double doors. "You're not to come in here unless he summons you."

With that, he knocked.

"Who is it?" a surprisingly refined voice replied: deep and clipped, carrying the sound of wealth.

"Luke, sir. I have Mr. Rawle's stepchildren." Luke offered an apologetic look to Caroline.

There was the scrape of a chair being pushed back. "Well then, do come in."

Luke opened one of the double doors and gestured for the two older girls to step inside, whilst he brought up the rear with Lambkin held snug against his chest. There was something endearing about the image, despite what Caroline and her sisters were about to face. Yes, she remained wary of Luke, but if Lambkin trusted him enough to sleep soundly, perhaps her wariness was misplaced.

Mr. Fox was not at all what Caroline had expected. Where she had envisioned a man as ugly as his deeds, wizened by his cruelty, his face and body corrupted by his wicked enterprises, she found a man of thirty or so, with sleek golden-blond hair, well-combed and oiled; attired in fine garments, and possessed of a jarringly pleasant face. Handsome, by anyone's standards; clean-shaven, his eyes a bright blue, his teeth straight and white as his mouth curved into an affable smile.

Those blue eyes settled instantly on Caroline. "Ladies, you are very welcome here."

"We didn't have much choice," Esther muttered.

Mr. Fox laughed. "Ah, I can see which one of you is the firebrand, but you need not fear me. If you are diligent, well-behaved ladies, you might find your lives very comfortable indeed." His gaze roved across Caroline, the corner of his mouth lifting in a way that made her uneasy. "How old are you?"

"Five-and ten," Caroline replied stiffly. "My sister is eleven. The baby is half a year."

Mr. Fox lounged in his high-backed chair. "And is the baby yours, Miss?"

"Mine?" Caroline choked. "Mercy, no! She is my sister."

"It had to be asked." He smirked. "You would not be the first young, unmarried mother to bring their child into my care."

Caroline straightened up. "Yes, well, that is not *my* situation. Our situation is that our stepfather wants to keep our mother from us, and us from her. He resents us, if that was not already obvious, and has sought a way to be rid of us without arousing suspicion. As such, I rather think we don't meet your criteria. You should give back the money that Quentin paid and let us go. We *have* a mother, and she will miss us if we don't return to her at once."

If Caroline had expected sympathy or any sort of understanding, she was sorely mistaken as an unpleasantly cheery laugh spilled from Mr. Fox's lips. In his blue eyes, there was a sly glint.

"You think I do not know who you are and why you are here?" he said, grinning. "Quentin Rawle is my more... 'respectable' cousin. He has been writing to me for months, telling me that he will be sending the three of you, but I was not certain it would happen. He kept delaying. I suppose he finally steeled his nerve."

Caroline gaped at the man. "You *know* him?"

"Indeed, just as I know that my cousin has been in love with that troublesome woman for years," Mr. Fox replied, as casually as if he was remarking upon the weather. "He has been after her since she began courting the man that I assume was your father—my cousin's former lodger. I forget the name."

Horror writhed in Caroline's stomach, hearing new meanings in things that Quentin had said over the years, whenever her family had encountered him. Indeed, just last year, in the gardens of Sadler's Wells, she remembered Quentin said, "Still the luckiest man in England, I see." She had assumed it was an awkward compliment, but now the memory carried a sinister undertone.

"Adam Calder," Caroline managed to rasp.

"Yes, that sounds about right." Mr. Fox took up a glass and sipped from it. "I always told Quentin that he needed to turn his attentions elsewhere, find himself a woman of station and wealth and good breeding, but it seems he was determined. He finally got what he wanted, I suppose. Much good it will do him. He will never be happy as second-best, but that is none of my business."

Feeling like she had suddenly been plunged underwater, submerged in the distressing revelations, Caroline's hand flew to her chest. She pressed her palm against the thud of her heart in a vain attempt to calm the rapid beats and ease the strain in her lungs, but it was no good.

Quentin planned this. Quentin must have been planning it for a long time, waiting for his moment. I bet he scoured the papers, eager to see my father's name in the obituaries. She felt sick, her mouth bone dry.

Turning her anger at Quentin towards his cousin, Caroline straightened up, glaring at the man behind the ornate mahogany desk. "No, Mr. Fox, it would appear that *your* business is holding babies hostage and exploiting children."

He laughed delightedly at that. "Perhaps, there are two firebrands in your family." His smile radiated menace.

"Your hair certainly suggests there is fire in you, Miss Caroline."

He knows our names. It is all true.

"But defiance and a sharp tongue will not serve you too well here," Mr. Fox continued, with a note of feigned regret. "You have been sold and bought, in essence. You are mine to do with as I please. If that is not enough motivation, then be assured that that child's comfort will depend on your compliance."

Caroline glanced at Lambkin, still sound asleep in Luke's care.

"Tomorrow," Mr. Fox said after a pointed pause, "Miss Esther will begin work at the textile mill. And you, Miss Caroline, will divide your time and attention between my mill and the other children in my care. At five-and-ten, you are the perfect age to be an excellent nanny. Plenty of vigour. And, quite fortunately, we have been in need of a new nanny for some weeks, so you have saved me the bother of finding a replacement."

Esther stared at the man, her mouth open, her eyes blank. "A... mill?"

"You will be taught what to do," Mr. Fox replied with a smile, taking another sip from his wine glass.

"And Lambkin?" Caroline asked.

Mr. Fox raised an eyebrow. "Lambkin?"

"The baby. What of the baby?"

He smirked and dabbed his mouth with a handkerchief. "If my cousin does not send any further coin when the time comes, you and I shall have to come to some arrangement. You might not be the child's mother, but you are the closest thing. As such, it will be your responsibility—your *choice*—what happens to her in due course."

An arrangement? Caroline's stomach lurched. A year ago,

her naivety would have rendered her oblivious to the man's meaning, but she was wise enough now to understand what Mr. Fox was suggesting. No matter what it took, or how much money she had to scrape together, she would never let that happen.

She caught Luke's eye, watching as he inclined his head, as if to say, *I meant what I said before—I'll help you.*

"The journey was long, Mr. Fox," Luke interjected. "I should show them to their quarters so they can get some sleep."

Mr. Fox nodded slowly, eyeing Luke with curiosity. "Yes, you do that. And you ladies really should get all the sleep that you can, for when tomorrow comes, you will need every wink of it."

CHAPTER 15

Luke wasted no time ushering the sisters out of the study, guiding them back through the draughty hallways until they came to a wide stairwell that snaked upwards, splitting off in two directions.

"The young'uns sleep separate to the help," Luke said apologetically, reaching the part of the staircase where the steps branched off, east and west. "And the help and young'uns sleep separate to the babies. If you stay here with Lambkin, I'll take Esther to where she needs to be."

"No," Caroline replied. "I'm coming with you."

Luke sighed. "Suit yourself."

As he pressed on, she gazed at the back of his head, where his golden hair curled at the nape of his neck. *Suit yourself...* She remembered those as his parting words in the apothecary, cursing herself for not realising that Luke's warning had gone deeper than the obvious. He had been trying to tell her that Quentin was not a good man, and she had trusted her father's judgment over his.

Presently, they came to a timeworn door, the paint

peeling on the wooden frame, the textured glass so cracked it almost looked like part of the design.

Luke opened it, revealing a dormitory of narrow, structurally suspect bunks. Peering over his shoulder, Caroline counted eight girls, while the rest of the beds lay stripped and empty.

"Mr. Luke!" one of the girls cried, scrambling down from her bed.

"Mr. Luke!" the rest chorused, rushing towards him. They were a mix of ages, from perhaps six to twelve, and each one seemed to adore Luke.

He laughed as they fought to hug him, fending them off with one arm outstretched. "I'm holding a baby, girls. I can't hug any of you right now." He paused, crouching down. "But I want you to take the very best care of my friend here—Esther. She's going to be staying here with you all, and I know you'll make her feel welcome. So, don't disappoint me."

Caroline frowned at him, surprised by the softness in his voice and the mirth in his expression. The boy she had known a year ago had not been capable of a true smile.

"Do I have to, Caro?" Esther whispered, slipping her hand into her sister's.

Caroline gave her hand a reassuring squeeze. "If those are the rules, we have to follow them." She leaned closer, lowering her voice so only Esther could hear. "It won't be forever, Estie. Just do what everyone else does until I can find a way to get us out of here. And, most of all, be brave. We'll only be apart at night, and you hate my snoring anyway."

A faint laugh escaped Esther's mouth. "It's not your snoring. You elbow me."

"Well then, you won't have to worry about that," Caroline urged. "You'll have a bed to yourself, and all of these girls to make friends with, who'll help you and keep you safe when I'm not here."

As if they had heard her, the other girls crowded around Esther, offering eager greetings and declarations of friendship. Clearly, they were trying to impress Luke, but if it meant that Esther would have an easier time, then Caroline did not mind the reason.

"You can sleep in the bed next to mine," one girl insisted, taking hold of Esther's hand and leading her towards a pleasant spot near to the windows.

Esther looked back as she followed the girl, putting on her bravest smile for her older sister. Caroline gave an encouraging nod, hoping fervently that—for her sisters, at least—what awaited them would not be so bad. True, it would never be the life they had enjoyed before, when their father was alive, but he had always encouraged them to be grateful, and to find beauty in each day, and to make the best of things. To do just that would be a fine way of honouring him.

"Let her settle in," Luke said quietly.

Caroline took a breath. "Where to next?"

"The nursery."

To her surprise, Luke took her by the hand and pulled her gently out of the room, perhaps knowing that she would not leave unless he made her. But he did not let go of her hand as they walked the chilly hallways, his calloused palm rough against her smooth palm. The texture spoke of a harder life than she could imagine, and stories that he had yet to tell her.

"Will she be all right with them?" Caroline asked, a little shy. "Are they... nice girls?"

Luke chuckled. "Half-wild, most of 'em, but they'll treat

her well. Soon enough, she'll be like a sister to them." A small line appeared between his eyebrows. "And they'll teach her what to do at the mill—keep an eye on her and that, so she doesn't come to any harm."

"Is it dangerous?" Without meaning to, she held onto his hand a bit tighter.

"Can be," he admitted. "But I'll be watching out for her too. Nothing bad will befall any one of you, so long as I'm here."

She cast a sideways glance at him, noting how much older he looked since the last time she had seen him. He had still been on the awkward brink between boyhood and manhood back then, but he had tipped towards the latter in the past year. He was taller, broader, filling out into a masculine physique, with a shadow of stubble across his defined jaw, the formerly soft edges of youth now hard and defined.

He was, in her opinion, far more handsome than his cousin once removed, Mr. Fox, their faint similarities undeniably more pleasing upon Luke's face.

"I never knew you had a heart a year ago," she teased mildly.

He shrugged, smiling. "It's amazing what you can find hidden underneath the machines at the mill."

As they walked on, coming to the staircase and heading up the opposite branch, Caroline almost began to believe the promise that Luke had made to help her.

"Are there no boys here?" she said, slowing her pace when he did, both approaching a door very similar to the one they had just left.

Luke tilted his head from side to side. "No older boys. They get sent off up to the mines when they're twelve or so. The younger ones are down that hallway there—just four of them, at present. Then there's girls and boys together in a room behind the nursery: all those from two to five. Not many at the moment." He pushed through the door. "And *this* is the nursery itself."

Caroline followed him in, her eyes widening. Five babies slept in rickety cradles in the centre of an otherwise sparse room, warmed by a meagre fireplace. Her heart ached for the slumbering babes, realising that each one had a family somewhere—a family that *might* come back for them one day, or might leave their fate to Mr. Fox.

There was a sixth cot standing empty, and as Caroline glanced at Lambkin, she knew precisely who that empty cot was for. After all, Quentin had written ahead.

"Luke, is that you?" a sharp voice called from a partially open doorway to the rear of the nursery. The room where the children aged two to five slept, presumably.

"It is, and I've got visitors," Luke replied.

An older woman emerged from the doorway, her dark eyes narrowing at Caroline. She could not have been older than fifty, her greying brown hair scraped back into the tightest of buns that made her seem doubly severe, yanking her eyebrows up into a constant expression of wary surprise. She was tall and stocky, thick arms testing the might of her dress's seams, her apron pulled high over an ample bosom. Rather frightening, if Caroline was being honest.

The woman looked Caroline up and down, then shrugged. "Put the littlun in the empty cradle. Girl or boy?"

"Girl," Luke replied. "Lambkin."

"Lambkin?" The woman sniffed. "Funny sort of name."

"My mama never got around to naming her," Caroline interjected defensively. "It's what we call her."

The woman nodded. "She need feeding?"

"No, she's had something to eat," Luke answered, putting Lambkin in Caroline's arms so that she could be the one to put the baby in the cradle.

"How old?" the woman asked.

"Half a year," Caroline said, wandering hesitantly towards the empty cradle. It seemed too cruel to just leave Lambkin there, so far from the warmth of her sisters, and the shared bed that she had known for the entirety of her short life.

The older woman made her way over, her voice gentler as she said, "She'll be safe with me, lass. I treat 'em all as me own." She set blankets down, but let Caroline tuck Lambkin in. "Besides, you'll be helping me, or so I hear. So, you'll see her plenty. Keep your chin up, eh."

"She's not mine," Caroline murmured, hearing the assumption in the woman's voice. "I'm just her sister."

The woman snorted. "No 'just' about it. Nothing so important as a sister."

Just then, Lambkin began to stir, her little face scrunching up in the way it did before she unleashed her most ear-splitting wails. The older nanny tutted under her breath, as if she—like Luke—knew the reason behind the baby's discomfort. But before either woman could do anything to soothe the child, Luke let Lambkin curl her hand around his finger, and started to sing.

He sang a sweet lullaby, his voice so melodic and charming that all the other babies seemed to sink deeper into their peaceful slumber. It was the most beautiful sound that Caroline had ever heard, bringing tears to her eyes as she listened, the fine hairs at the back of her neck prickling, her heart slowing as if she, too, was about to be lulled to sleep.

"What have I told you about interfering?" the older woman scolded, with the faintest hint of a smile.

Luke grinned back at her and kept singing, his perfect voice smoothing out the wrinkles of Lambkin's displeasure, averting the screams that had surely been close to erupting from her tiny body.

"He does this a lot?" Caroline could not help but ask.

The older woman nodded. "He can't be stopped. I'd try harder to kick him out if his singing wasn't the only thing that can get some of these babies to sleep at times."

Luke continued to smile as he sang, and as Lambkin fell into a peaceful slumber of her own, Caroline caught him looking at her. His grey eyes were warm despite their steely colour, and when he nudged her sharply in the ribs with his elbow, she found that she could not resist. Though her voice was not nearly as wondrous as Luke's, Caroline heard herself joining in, the two of them singing a lullaby for all the babies with uncertain futures, to make them feel safe, if just for a while.

CHAPTER 16

Two Years Later...

Warm summer sunlight pierced the long windows of the mill, ratcheting up the temperature inside, until it was as insufferably balmy as a greenhouse. Movements were sluggish, the golden light catching the miasma of fabric motes that drifted and swirled in the molasses-thick air, the constant motion of the clattering machines making it all the hotter.

Sweat beaded on Caroline's brow, droplets trickling down the collar of her dress as she ran the length of the textile mill, weaving in and out of those who were still at their work. She gained a few sharp looks and sharper words, apologising as she hurried on to fetch Esther.

"Estie!" Caroline crouched low, squinting underneath the industrial loom that turned the raw threads of wool and cotton into reams of fabric.

She hated that her sister had to work beneath the looms —the most dangerous job in the entire mill, some would say—but Esther was small and skinny for her age, getting skinnier by the month, so the overseers kept putting her under.

Esther crawled along, the sight of her like a breath of fresh air after a long, humid day.

"I thought you'd forgotten about me," she said as she ducked under the thick edge of the machine and got to her feet, dusting off the detritus that had gathered on her clothes: clumps of dust and fibres and threads that had fallen loose.

"As if I would," Caroline replied, grabbing her sister's hand.

Together, they hurried out of the mill, their shifts at an end. They crossed the dirty yard where carts waited to take away the fabrics, waving to friends and acquaintances who were just heading into the mill to start the afternoon shift. *Their* expressions were far less enthusiastic, for they would work until midnight—longer if it was demanded.

"I doubt I'll need anything to eat tonight," Esther said, the sisters slowing their pace as they left the high walls of the mill yard and turned onto the street. "I'm certain I've swallowed my weight in dust."

Caroline glanced down at her sister. "You need to tie something around your face. It'll keep out the fibres."

"I can't breathe when I do that," Esther protested, sucking in a deep lungful of the sticky summer air. The inhale ended in a spluttering cough that worried Caroline, but Esther recovered quickly, skipping along as if it had never happened.

Despite how skinny and exhausted they were, worn to the bone by the exertions of the mill, a giddiness soon bloomed between the sisters with every step they put between themselves and that place.

Heading down a slightly sloping hill towards the centre

of the city, Caroline gasped as a shadowy figure stepped out of an alleyway.

She smacked the figure in the arm. "Luke! Don't do that! I thought you were a thief!"

"And I thought you said you'd be out by three o'clock," Luke replied gruffly, shoving his hands into the pockets of his waistcoat.

Out in the world, he was as unsmiling as she had remembered him to be, three years ago, but she had come to learn that it was just a façade. Inside the place they all called home, he transformed, his demeanour cheerful and lively, with smiles for all the children who adored him... and for Caroline, too.

"It is barely half-past," Caroline chided mildly.

"And half an hour is longer than you'd think when you're the one waiting." He cast her a sideways glance, a glimmer of the true Luke shining in his grey eyes.

Esther weaved her arm through his. "Don't quarrel, you two. I can't bear it when you argue."

Caroline laughed, taking hold of Esther's other arm as they ventured further into the city, a weight lifting off her shoulders for a while. There was nothing so freeing as walking away from the mill with her sister and Luke, for she could trick herself into thinking that they would keep walking, never to return to that place.

A short while later, they came to a quaint little shop, painted a mossy green. Brightly coloured wooden toys seemed to peer out of the bay window, whilst children peered in, pressing their noses to the pane and pleading with parents and nannies to go inside.

"Here." Luke drew a limp pouch from his pocket and put it into Caroline's hand.

She frowned at it. "What's this?"

"Money for Lambkin's gift," he replied flatly, as if it should have been obvious.

"I can't take this. I have the money I need."

Luke shook his head. "You don't. You have money that ought to go to Mr. Fox. If you spend it here, you'll be scrabbling and scraping to make up the deficit, and I'd rather you didn't." He shrugged. "Means I'll have to work extra hours in the nursery. This way, I won't have to."

Caroline hesitated, seeing the generosity beneath the nonchalance. He did that often, sneaking additional coins into her secret cache, buying things she had mentioned she needed, appearing out of nowhere when she was on her way to purchase something for herself or Esther or Lambkin. Sometimes, she pretended not to notice, especially if it was a month where she had not made enough to pay Mr. Fox for Lambkin's keep, but she tried to protest wherever she could.

"So, this is to help *you*?" she asked, her eyebrow raised.

Luke nodded. "Exactly."

"Caro, just take it," Esther urged. "We'll be late if we don't hurry."

Caroline could not deny that she was rather glad she would not have to spend every hour God gave in the streets of Leeds, gathering up the scraps that seemed useless, but could be sold at a meagre price to the right buyer: bits of ribbon, cigar ends, the occasional dropped piece of silver or jewellery, pieces of string and twine.

Still, it was the only way she could make the money she needed to keep Lambkin safe. She had tried working in a public house, but Mr. Fox had found out and punished her, calling it an insult to his good name for one of his wards to be working in such a place. She had tried selling pies at the market, with the same result. She had tried everything short of the only thing she would not do, and picking was the sole occupation that Mr. Fox could not stop.

"Thank you, Luke," Caroline said softly, spurred on by a sudden boldness to show her gratitude as well as speak it.

Leaning forward, she kissed him on the cheek... and was immediately overwhelmed with embarrassment. To hide it, she hurried into the shop with the coin pouch in hand, not daring to look back and see the expression on Luke's face.

"I'm watchin' you," the proprietor warned from behind the counter. "Don't think I won't send for the constables if I see you touchin' aught you shouldn't be."

Caroline smiled politely. "I just want that duck."

She pointed to a small wooden duck on wheels, painted in blues and greens and reds. She had seen another child playing with it; the duck was attached to a string, making its head moved when it was pulled along. The sort of toy that would delight Lambkin, but it was also an homage to their father: his little ducks, surviving together.

The proprietor frowned and stuck out her hand. "Money first."

"Of course." Caroline walked over and counted out the coins from Luke's pouch, remembering a time when sellers like this would have fallen over themselves to receive her custom; how they had fawned over her father, giving away things for free just to be able to say that they were favoured by the famous Adam Calder.

"Stay here. I'll fetch it. Don't touch anythin' else," the cantankerous woman grumbled, coming out from behind the counter.

She took the duck from its position in the window and brought it over, reluctantly wrapping it in brown paper, tying it with a plain string bow, before handing it to Caroline.

"Go on," the woman muttered. "Off with you."

Caroline held the package to her chest. "Thank you."

Heartened despite the unpleasant exchange, she made her way out of the shop... and remembered what she had done. Luke could not look her in the eyes, an awkward smile upon his lips, whilst Esther grinned delightedly at his side.

"He went so red, Caro!" Esther teased. "I didn't know a person could turn that colour."

Luke shot her a look. "It's hot, Estie. Everyone is red in the face."

"Not as red as you," Esther replied, giggling.

Luke cleared his throat. "Did you get the duck?"

"I got the duck," Caroline confirmed, noticing a trace of pink still lingering in Luke's cheeks.

"Come on, then," he said stiffly. "We have precious cargo to deliver."

"Aren't you going to kiss him again, Caro?" Esther grinned, evidently enjoying herself.

This time, it was Caroline who shot her sister a warning look. "Behave yourself. It was a gesture of gratitude. People do it all the time."

"Not that I've seen," Esther insisted, shrugging. "But you pretend you don't adore one another if it makes you feel better. I'll just patiently wait for the day you end up marrying each other."

"Estie!" Caroline choked.

"What?" Esther smirked.

Luke rolled his eyes. "You've clearly inhaled too much of the dye at the mill."

He started walking, and the sisters had no choice but to follow, half-running to catch up to him as they made their way back to Fox House: The 'baby farm' and profitable orphanage that they reluctantly called home. Yet, most of the time, it was not nearly as much of a prison as Quentin's townhouse had been.

* * *

"Mr. Luke!" a horde of children chorused. "Miss Caro!"

Esther pulled a face as she entered the main hall next to Caroline and Luke. "And what about me?"

"Estie!" the children duly cried, rushing towards the trio.

Opening out their arms, Caroline and Luke embraced the eager children, swinging them around, tickling them, complimenting them, allowing them to climb all over them. Much to the distaste of the 'Mothers' who sat at the long table in the hall, where dinner was usually served.

They were not really mothers—at least not to any of the children at Fox House—but they were the paid women who 'adopted' or 'fostered' the babies who ended up in Mr. Fox's so-called care. After all, suspicions would be aroused if Mr. Fox 'adopted' them all himself, though there was no mistaking who got the lion's share of the income. Indeed, the 'Mothers' were just names on a document, really, who occasionally came by to receive their payment from Mr. Fox. Money for their silence, nothing more.

Luke and Caroline, and the older nanny, Rosemary, were more like parents to the children than any of the 'Mothers' would ever be. The only reason the 'Mothers' were happy that their fosters were alive was because their money would come to an end if the child died.

"Everyone sit down," Luke said, pointing to the table. "I've got a surprise for you all."

"A surprise?" one of the children asked. "What surprise?"

Luke leaned in, putting a finger to his lips. "We're going to have a party."

"A party?" a different child shrieked excitedly.

Luke nodded. "For Lambkin's birthday." She paused. "Does anyone know where Lambkin is?"

Caroline searched the sweltering hall, unease knotting in her stomach when she could not find her littlest sister. It was a persistent plague of a fear, striking every time she went to the mills or spent hours scouring the streets for anything of value; forever afraid that she would return to Fox House to discover that Lambkin had been taken away or worse.

At that moment, Rosemary entered the hall through a door at the back, sweating profusely, her face blotchy and red from the heat of the day, made worse by the stoves and steam of the kitchens. Riding on her back, safe and sound, was Lambkin.

"Someone looking for this little rascal?" Rosemary said, setting the little girl down.

Relief washed over Caroline in a cooling wave, her lungs drawing in a relaxed breath. "I hope you've not been pestering Rosemary?"

"*Helping* Rosemary!" Lambkin insisted, running across the flagstone floor and into Caroline's open arms.

"I've made a birthday dinner," Rosemary said with a fond smile, for though she would never admit that she had favourites, Lambkin had made her mark upon the older woman's heart. All of them had. And Rosemary, in turn, had left a mark upon the hearts of the three sisters, becoming the kindly grandmother that they had never known.

Still, the making of the birthday dinner was not

unusual; the older woman did it for everyone, even those who did not know the date of their birthdays. She simply made one up for them and, from then on, it became their birthday. Caroline always looked forward to such days.

Lambkin kissed Caroline's cheek. "I helped Rosemary."

"Did you now?" Caroline beamed, hugging the little girl tightly.

Luke put his fingers to his lips and whistled loudly, snaring the attention of all the children in one fell swoop. "Right, you bunch of urchins! Wash your hands, set the table, and let us have ourselves a lovely party!"

Laughing merrily, the children obeyed him, darting off to scrub their dirty hands, splitting the responsibility of putting bowls and cutlery on the long table, everyone climbing into their respective seats in readiness for the dinner Rosemary had prepared.

Meanwhile, the grim-faced 'Mothers' made themselves scarce, retreating to a room on the other side of the hall that no one was allowed to enter but them. Judging by the aroma of tobacco and stale liquor that drifted out whenever the door opened, Caroline could guess what went on in there. Once, she had glimpsed a bottle of that wretched laudanum, providing an explanation for the vacant look that many of the women had when they emerged from that room again.

With the unpleasant women gone, it was not long before a celebratory air filled the cavernous hall, the children permitted to be themselves now they were out from under the disdainful observation of those vultures. Laughter, jokes, stories—the chaotic babble of it raised up to the rafters, swelling Caroline's heart as she took her seat between her sisters, Luke sitting opposite.

Lambkin sat in pride of place at the head of the table,

where she stared wide-eyed at the hearty portion of meat stew that Rosemary ladled out for her. She received extra potatoes and roasted carrots too, and though it was perhaps far too hot for such a meal, *all* the children tucked in as if they had not eaten in weeks.

"It was a good day, the day you were born," Rosemary remarked to Lambkin, as she sat down beside Luke. "Don't you ever forget that, sweet girl."

Lambkin grinned through a mouthful of bread and stew, her big eyes alight with a happiness that Caroline wished would stay there forever.

"Eat up," Rosemary said, nodding to Caroline's untouched plate.

Snapping out of her pleased trance, Caroline did just that, savouring every mouthful. The lamb was tender, falling apart in the rich broth; the carrots and turnips were soft and sweet and earthy, the bread warm and fresh as she dipped it into the stew. The potatoes were golden and buttery, the roasted carrots so perfectly honeyed that it made her mouth tingle.

"One of your best, Rosemary," Luke said with a wink.

Rosemary elbowed him in the arm. "Take your mischief elsewhere."

"What? I mean it. It's one of your best." He smiled, completely at ease within the confines of Fox House. "But I hope you didn't make much for pudding. I took the liberty."

Caroline frowned at him from across the table. "What do you mean?"

"You'll see," Luke replied, meeting her eyes for a moment.

Caroline's cheeks warmed as she remembered the press of his soft skin against her lips, hardly able to believe that she had been so daring. His lopsided smile seemed to suggest that he was thinking of the same moment, prompting her to lower her gaze back to her delicious dinner.

He stayed true to his word as everyone finished their meal, mopping up the last of the stew with whatever bread remained. He slunk away from the table and slipped through the door at the back of the hall, returning a few minutes later with a cake, adorned with four little candles—one for each of the years that Lambkin had lived, and a fourth that represented the hope that she would live at least one more. He cupped his hand around them to stop them from sputtering out and carefully set the cake in front of Lambkin.

"Make a wish," he said with a smile, stepping back.

All of the children stared enviously at Lambkin, a few of them trying to blow a breath up the table to take the wish for themselves.

Lambkin squeezed her eyes shut, her mouth moving silently, and when she opened them again, she expelled a mighty breath that blew out all four at once.

"What did you wish for?" one of the children shouted.

Lambkin smiled. "Not telling."

"That's not fair!" a different child complained. "Tell us what you wished for!"

"No," Lambkin replied simply, as thin threads of smoke wisped upwards from the blown-out candles.

To avoid further quarrel, Caroline took that moment to bring out the brown-paper package from the toy shop. "This is from all of us," she said, sliding the parcel to Lambkin.

Clapping her hands excitedly, Lambkin carefully undid the bow of string and unfurled the gift as if it was the most precious thing in all the world. As the first flash of colour emerged, she shrieked with glee, the sight and sound of her joy rising higher and higher as she revealed the duck.

"Thank you, Caro!" Lambkin cried. "Thank you, Estie! Thank you, Mr. Luke! Thank you, Rosemary! Thank you, everyone!"

Some of the children nodded as if they had purchased the duck with their own coin, whilst others gazed adoringly at the colourful toy, and a few others had a jealous look about them. They need not have worried; Lambkin would share the toy, for that was the way she had been raised at Fox House. Nothing truly belonged to anyone, everything shared and played with communally—though that was not to say that it did not sometimes cause fights amongst them.

"Who wants cake?" Luke asked, plucking off the candles.

Twenty-three hands shot up, including Esther and Lambkin, the eagerness of the youngest reflected in the oldest. Even the two boys of twelve-years-old who would soon be taken away to the mines in the north squirmed desperately in their chairs, stretching their arms as high as they could, offering a flash of the innocent boyhood that the mines would undoubtedly stamp out of them.

Luke laughed. "Does anyone *not* want cake?"

All the hands went down, and with a smile on his face, Luke cut the cake into twenty-five perfect slices—small, but more than enough for the children who rarely had the chance to eat a piece of cake.

"There's one missing," Caroline pointed out, when only two slices remained and neither she nor Rosemary nor Luke had a piece.

Luke waved a dismissive hand. "I don't like cake. These are for you and Rosemary."

"Nonsense," Rosemary protested. "There's not a bit of cake that has ever been safe from you, Luke."

He shrugged. "I ate too much of your delicious stew."

He pushed the last two pieces towards the women, and began to clear the table before they could insist on him having some. Caroline watched him with curiosity as she took a bite of the sweet, buttery cake, filled with a tart berry jam.

"Should I save him some anyway?" she asked Rosemary.

The older woman chuckled. "He won't take it if you do. He's a strange one, that boy." She cast Caroline a pointed look. "But he's a good lad. You could do far worse."

Caroline's eyes widened. "I don't know what you mean," she spluttered, returning to her cake, concentrating on it so intently that she could have counted every seed within the jam.

Meanwhile, Rosemary laughed softly, the sound warming Caroline's cheeks until they were undoubtedly bright red.

CHAPTER 17

The good cheer of the birthday party could not, and did not, last beyond the evening. The next day, everything was as it always was. The children had eaten a meagre breakfast of thin porridge, scrubbed their faces and hands pink, and been herded out of the door by Caroline and Luke, so they would not be late to the mill.

It was an insufferably hot day, the mill sweltering, the air so thick it cloyed in the lungs, and with heat like that came accidents. Everyone was slower, less alert, and Caroline had learned that she needed to keep a closer eye on the children she felt responsible for.

"Counting again?" Luke asked, as he walked by her at luncheon.

All of the workers were given half an hour for luncheon or dinner, depending on their shift. They received a bowl of watery soup apiece, and some stale bread on a good day, and it served as Caroline's one opportunity to count the children and make sure no one was missing.

"Someone has to," she replied with a smile.

"All six-and-ten?"

She flashed him a mock-withering look. "That's not at all amusing."

Nevertheless, she doubted herself for a moment. There were only five-and-ten children from Fox House at the mill that day. At least, she thought that was right.

"Sorry." He smiled and sat down. "Not a helpful jest."

"No, it's not." She counted the children again, just to be sure. They were all accounted for—mostly girls, all between the ages of six and four-and-ten.

As the children ate their luncheon, Caroline's heart weighed heavy. There should have been more children around that rickety table, despite the awful circumstances. There should have been more children at Fox House who were not there anymore: sold or sent away or kicked out or worse by Mr. Fox, when they grew too old for him to maintain the ruse of an orphanage. Indeed, Caroline knew that she was a rare exception, making it to seven-and-ten without being dismissed to the workhouse or to fend for herself.

"What's that face for?" Luke asked, frowning at her.

Caroline shook her head, scooping up a spoonful of watery broth. "Nothing. Just thinking."

"About what?"

"It doesn't matter," she lied.

Within her first few months at Fox House, she had learned what happened to the babies when the mothers or families stopped paying for their care. In winter, they were left in a storage room with the windows wide open. In the warmer months, they were simply neglected and left to die. At least, that was what was *supposed* to happen, but Rosemary and Luke had come up with an alternative scheme, not long after he had arrived at Fox House.

He took the baby away, claiming to Mr. Fox that it had

died, gave a signal to Rosemary, and slipped out into the night, leaving the child on the doorstep of a church or a true orphanage. What happened after that, no one knew. They could only hope.

"Tell me anyway," Luke insisted softly, his grey eyes twinkling with that warmth that she had come to cherish.

She puffed out a breath. "I was just wondering where the children are."

"Which children?" He frowned.

"The ones who aren't here," she replied sadly. "I can't help it—I think about them a lot: if they're happy, if they're healthy, if they're even alive. If they're... better off where they are." She shook her head. "It's silly. We'll never know, so what's the use?"

"It's not silly." He reached beneath the table and took hold of her hand, squeezing it gently. "I think about them too. If I did the right thing or if I just tossed them from the frying pan into the fire, you know?"

She nodded, understanding perfectly.

"But I tell myself that at least I gave them a chance," he added. "That's all anyone can hope for, really."

She smiled, her response interrupted by the sound of coughing, coming from a few of the children: a hacking, wrenching cough that had become more noticeable of late. It worried her, but it was not as if she could summon a physician. Mr. Fox would never allow it. Why would he, when he did not care? He could always acquire more children, more free labour, more chattel for his baby farm.

"Remember to keep cloths wrapped around your mouths," she said to the children, already certain that they would not heed her. It was too stifling to cover their mouths, especially underneath the machinery.

"If I see one of you not following Miss Caro's instructions, I won't sing you a song tonight," Luke warned, sparking Caroline's admiration.

Grumbling and groaning amongst themselves, the children drew out the cloths they had shoved into pockets and aprons. Still, Caroline knew they would only keep them on for a while before the discomfort placed the cloths firmly back into hiding.

"Thank you," she murmured.

"Don't thank me." He smiled. "You know they won't do as they're told for long."

She mustered a sad laugh and spooned up another mouthful of broth. She was just about to swallow it down, when the door to the makeshift dining hall burst open, the old hinges squealing. Everyone's attention snapped towards it, tense silence spreading across the gathering of workers. Mr. Fox's right-hand man—a reed-thin, unpleasant weasel called Mr. Haugh—stood there, glaring at the workers with his beady little eyes.

"Miss Caroline Rawle," he said curtly, seeking her out. "Mr. Fox wants to see you immediately."

Caroline bristled, hating the sound of that name—a name that was not, and never would be, hers. Mr. Fox did it on purpose; she was certain of that. Just as he summoned her to his office on a whim to irritate her, disturbing what little peace she could gain from her life at the mill and Fox House.

"Do you want me to come with you?" Luke whispered.

Caroline shook her head. "It won't make a difference. It never does."

She hated it when Mr. Fox did this, but it no longer surprised or alarmed her. He liked to steal any opportunity to get her alone, though it was far worse at Fox House where it was not so public. *Then,* she liked to have Luke nearby, or Rosemary.

Thus far, no real harm had come to her—just the threat of it.

"I won't be far away," Luke promised, regardless.

Leaving what was left of her broth, Caroline got to her feet, ignoring the stares and whispers of the other workers as she walked to Mr. Haugh. He turned his nose up at her and twisted around, marching back the way he had come, simply expecting her to follow behind.

She trailed the weedy man through the din and dust of the mill floor, the machines never stopping, spooling out ream after ream of textiles that would go on to become a thousand different things. The workers sweated over their back-breaking work, their own clothes soaked through, their eyes glassy as if their minds were somewhere else entirely. A recipe for disaster, in truth, but she could not help everyone. She could barely help herself.

At the end of the huge machine hall, creaky metal stairs led up to a mezzanine, and the door to Mr. Fox's office. It stood open and he stood waiting for her, leaning against the front of his desk, a sly smile upon his lips.

"I trust I was not disturbing your luncheon?" he asked, his blue eyes glinting.

"Not at all," Caroline replied politely.

"Well, do not stand out there all afternoon," he said, beckoning. "In you come. Mr. Haugh, if you would not mind closing the door."

Mr. Fox's manservant obeyed without hesitation, the *click* of the door in the jamb sending a shudder down Caroline's spine. The way he stood right in front of it, his back to the two rectangular windows in the door, added a fresh shiver of unease.

"After all you did for your darling sister yesterday," Mr. Fox said, "*I* have a gift for *you*."

He wandered past her and slowly pulled the blinds closed, taking his time to blot out the foggy light that filtered in from the mill. All that remained was the sickly glow of two lanterns that he had on his desk, and the feeling that, after two years of avoiding the worst, Caroline was well and truly trapped.

CHAPTER 18

Like his namesake, Mr. Fox prowled back and forth in front of Caroline, putting himself between her and the door. Although, she was not sure what good it would have done if she had been able to make it out of the office, not with Mr. Fox's minion standing right there.

"It does not please me to mention it," Mr. Fox finally spoke, "but you will soon be eight-and-ten."

"In half a year," she pointed out stiffly, uncertain of where he was going with the conversation.

He cast her a sharp look: a warning not to interrupt him again. "Once you reach that age, you can no longer remain under my roof," he continued. "I have already allowed you to remain long after I should have done."

"I am not leaving my sisters," Caroline replied regardless, holding her nerve.

Mr. Fox smiled coldly. "No, I thought not. With that in mind, I have an offer for you."

He waited for a moment, no doubt wanting her to ask what that offer might be. She did not give him the satisfaction, waiting silently, patiently. Any words that might have come out of her mouth in that instant would have trembled, so it was better not to say anything at all.

"You could remain at Fox House as a true nursemaid to the babies in my care," he said, his mouth twisting in faint annoyance. "In order to do that, of course, you would need to be with-child. You would need to have the ability to be a wet nurse to the babies. It would be of great benefit to me, in truth. And, naturally, such a child would be well taken care of, and if it was a son, I would raise him as if he were legitimate."

Horror frothed in Caroline's veins, bubbling into her chest where it transformed into a sharp burn. Acid seared up her throat, robbing her of her ability to speak, whilst her eyes bulged in disgust at the proposition.

There were other young women who came to Fox House to feed the babies, but they were paid in gin and laudanum, desperate to escape their own lives for a while. They did not stay at Fox House, they did not have their babies in that place; they came in, did their task, and left. And when their milk ran dry, others were found.

"No," Caroline wheezed, sick to her stomach at the very thought of what he was obviously suggesting. "Never."

Mr. Fox clicked his tongue. "Do not be hasty, Caroline. Think of Lambkin. Perhaps, her care could be part of the offer—I know how hard you have worked to pay me for her upkeep. Think what you could do with all of that income if you did not have to pay me anymore."

"Never," Caroline repeated, her voice a hissing rasp. "I have paid for my sister, and I will continue to pay for my sister, with coin and nothing more."

Mr. Fox sighed, shaking his head. "I had hoped that the last two years had taught you how to be reasonable, and how to appreciate my generosity." He took a step closer to her. "I know how you are gaining the coin to pay for your sister. What I am offering is far more agreeable, yet not much different to what you are already doing. Or do you prefer selling yourself? Would you rather do that until you are utterly ruined, instead of spending a few nights with me?"

"What?" Caroline took a sharp intake of breath. "I haven't sold myself to anyone, and I don't intend to start now."

"You would lie to me?"

She frowned, confused. "I'm not lying. I have never sold myself! I search the streets for cigar ends and ribbons and anything else I can find. I don't... do anything like you are suggesting!"

"And I do not believe you," he whispered. "There is no possible way you could keep paying me, if that was all you were doing. I see you sneak out in the middle of the night. I see you sneak in at dawn. I *know* what you are doing!"

"You don't! Evidently, you don't!" she tried to argue, but the rest of her protest became an almighty scream as Mr. Fox lunged forward, grabbing her by the arms.

He pushed her backwards until the small of her back hit the edge of his mahogany desk, a yelp of pain dulling the edges of her scream. She was swamped by the height and breadth of him pressing down on her, forcing her spine to bend in ways it was not meant to as he attempted to pin her on the surface of the desk.

She clawed at him, tried to kick out at him; she wriggled and she writhed, but he had become immoveable, his strength overwhelming her with ease. He did not seem to notice or care that she was in pain, his blue eyes gleaming with menace, and one sole intention.

Just then, the office door flew inward. Mr. Haugh lay in a spluttering heap on the ground, holding his stomach, and Luke stood there in the doorway, wielding a length of wood.

"Let go of her," Luke spat. "Let go of her, right now."

Esther ran in behind him, unleashing a horrified gasp. "Unhand my sister!"

A snarl rumbled in Mr. Fox's throat as he stepped back, but not before giving Caroline a shove of irritation. But as he turned to face Luke and Esther, his expression became a mask of cool calm, his hands raised up in a gesture of mock surrender.

"What nonsense is this?" he asked. "Miss Caroline fell and caught her. As you can see, she is perfectly safe. The same, however, cannot be said for the two of you—what right do you think you have to barge into my private office without my permission?"

Luke held up the length of wood, his eyes narrowed. "You don't fool me, Mr. Fox. I know what you were doing. Step away from her."

"I am a gentleman, Luke," Mr. Fox retorted with a tone of disgust. "I do not know what went on where you were raised, but *I* was not raised so despicably. There will be punishment for this. For both of you. Indeed, because of this transgression, Miss Esther, you can be the reason that the fee of care for your little sister has just gone up."

He smoothed his hands down the front of his waistcoat and clawed his fingertips through his hair, taking a breath before he marched right past Luke and Esther, and out of the door. His footsteps clanked on the mezzanine and continued on down the staircase, offering no assistance to Mr. Haugh as he went.

"Are you well?" Luke dropped the length of wood and

ran to Caroline, heaving her up off the desk and pulling her close, holding her to him as if he never intended to let her go again. "Did he hurt you?" he murmured, cradling the back of her head. "Did he do anything to you?"

Caroline did not know whether to burst into tears or hold Luke in return.

"Tell me you are all right," he urged, curving himself around her as if that would be enough to keep her safe. "Tell me he didn't touch you."

She swallowed past the lump in her throat. "He... made me... a terrible offer, but... he didn't harm me." Her breath hitched. "You got here... in time."

"Esther, fetch some tea from the dining hall," Luke instructed, as he pulled back, caressing Caroline's cheek, brushing the hair out of her face.

He searched her face as if he did not believe her words, his other arm encircling her waist, keeping her upright as he looked for the truth in her eyes. Meanwhile, Esther hurried back out to do as she had been asked, leaving the pair alone in the gloomy office.

"What offer did he make?" Luke asked, scooping her to him again, hugging her so tightly that she could not breathe and did not want to.

She held him in return, clinging to him with sudden desperation. "He wants... me to be a nursemaid." Her voice caught in her throat. "But I know his meaning—he wants to... me to have a child, *his* child, and won't stop until he has what he wants. It's why he has kept me around for so long. I was never an exception, just... part of a plan."

"I won't let it happen," Luke growled, his cheek against hers. "I swear to you, I won't let it happen. I'll protect you. I promise."

As he held her and she held him back, she had no doubt

that he wanted to keep that promise, and would do everything within his power to see her protected, but Mr. Fox was too wily, too clever, and too determined. He would find a way; he had already begun to, for how was she supposed to pay more for Lambkin when she could barely scrape together the current sum?

Everything she had built for herself and her sisters in Leeds, everything she had worked so hard for in that city, everything she had put in place to keep her family safe was unravelling before her eyes.

"What if you can't?" she whispered, her heart sore.

He embraced her even tighter, murmuring against her neck, "I'll think of something, Caro. If it's the last thing I do, I'll think of something."

Burying her face in his shoulder, she wished more than anything that she could believe him.

CHAPTER 19

Caroline's nerves teetered on a knife edge with every day that passed after the incident in the office. From the moment she woke at dawn and prepared for work at the mill to the moment she went to bed after picking the streets until gone midnight, she waited for the axe to fall.

The waiting, it seemed, was the worst part; her anxiety reaching unbearable heights. She was short-tempered with the children, kept making small mistakes at the machines, and could not sleep even when her body was beyond exhausted: a shadow of herself.

But a week went by and still nothing had come of the incident. Mr. Fox did not bother her at the mill and had been absent from Fox House since that day, and as the next week began, Caroline could not help but feel a semblance of normality returning.

It helped that Luke was never far from her, keeping his promise to protect her, watching over her as often as he could.

"What are you doing out here?" Luke asked, his body half out of the arched doorway that led into the yard of Fox House. It was filled with broken furniture, crumbling apple crates, random lengths of wood, and piles of rubble and glass that made it no safe place for children to play.

Caroline tilted her face up to the warm noonday sun. "Enjoying this beautiful Sunday."

"Out here, though?" Amusement lilted in his voice.

"I knew I wouldn't be troubled."

He chuckled softly. "Ah, so I'm troubling you? You know, it's not so easy to keep an eye on you when you sneak away like this."

"I had a feeling you'd find me," she replied, as he sat down beside her. "How simple do you think it would be to clear away all of this?"

Luke gave a low whistle. "Not simple at all. Besides, Mr. Fox would never allow it."

Caroline shuddered at the sound of that man's name. "It would be nice, though, wouldn't it? For the children."

"I suppose it would," Luke replied. "I've never thought of it before."

They sat like that, arm to arm, thigh to thigh, shoulder to shoulder, gazing out at the debris of the yard. Being Sunday, there was no work to be done, other than the chores that had already been completed, and Rosemary was in the kitchens making one of her famous rabbit stews for the large household. Where the rabbits had come from, no one asked, and she did not tell. They ate heartily and did not need to know anything beyond that.

"Thank you," Caroline said quietly.

Luke cast her a sideways glance. "What for? I haven't done anything other than bother you."

"You've done far more than that," she chided playfully,

her cheeks warming. "I never properly thanked you for what you did at the mill, and I haven't exactly been pleasant since. So... thank you for what you did. Thank you for rescuing me and thank you for keeping your promise."

He dropped his chin to his chest, a strangely sad expression washing over his face. "You shouldn't thank me."

"Well, tough, because I am," she insisted, nudging him lightly in the ribs.

He nudged her back. "In that case, stop sneaking away from me."

"I can't promise that." She laughed. "Sometimes, I need a moment to myself. I adore those children in there, but there are occasions where I need to not be climbed all over, and..."

She trailed off, something shifting in the air between her and Luke. He was looking at her, not with the need to protect, but with an intensity she had not seen since he held her a week ago. Her face flushed with warmth, fighting the urge to turn her gaze away.

His hand came up to touch her warm cheek, his thumb brushing the rosy apple.

"What are you doing?" she whispered, not wanting to shatter the moment.

"Just looking at you," he replied. "Keeping an eye on you."

She smiled. "Is this to keep me from slinking out of your sight?"

"Perhaps." He leaned closer, his gaze flitting from her eyes to her lips.

Her heart thudded wildly in her chest as he bent his head, his mouth so close to hers that she could feel the tickle of his breath against her lips.

Luke was going to kiss her.

With a soft smile, he leaned ever closer, and as she closed her eyes and tilted her head up slightly, his lips grazed hers. A sweet, hesitant brush that made her feel as if she had been beneath the summer sun for hours: tingly and feverish, in the best possible way.

"Mr. Luke! Miss Caro!" an excited voice yelled, jolting the pair apart as if they had sat upon a piece of broken glass.

A small child darted out of the doors and down the steps, skidding to a halt in front of Caroline and Luke—entirely oblivious to what he had just interrupted. He wore a giddy smile, pointing frantically back at Fox House, so out of puff that he could not get his words out.

"What is it, Frankie?" Luke asked impatiently.

The boy stooped to catch his breath, still pointing. "There's a... show on the Green."

"Pardon?" Caroline stared at the boy.

"Performers... with puppets," the boy wheezed. "Out on the Green."

Caroline and Luke exchanged a bemused look. 'The Green' was nothing more than the barren square of land between the buildings where Fox House was situated, and —as far as Caroline knew—had never been used for anything except dumping refuse and unwanted things, or as an impromptu bed for drunkards who had tripped on said refuse and were too inebriated to get up until they had sobered. Now and then, the children of Fox House would play games with the children of the cramped houses around the square, but that was a rare thing indeed.

"Are you sure?" Caroline asked.

The boy nodded eagerly. "Everyone is going out to watch before dinner. You have to come too. I was sent to fetch you."

He lunged forwards and grabbed Caroline and Luke by the hand, pulling them insistently towards the door. With a respective groan, the pair got up and followed the boy through Fox House and out of the main entrance, into the street.

In that grey and dismal patch of nothing, where no trees or shrubs dared to grow save for browned weeds, they were surprised to find that it was not a figment of a child's wild imagination; there *was* some manner of performance afoot.

A colourful structure had been erected, red velvet curtains opened to reveal puppets who were in the midst of whacking each other with bats, much to the raucous delight of the children who sat cross-legged on the ground. There was an entire crowd, pooled together from the buildings that surrounded the square, all laughing and applauding together.

"And here I was, thinking Frankie was just looking for an excuse to interrupt," Luke said quietly, discreetly slipping his hand into Caroline's.

She blushed furiously, searching the crowd of children to make sure that none of those under her care had noticed. Esther was seated near the back with her arm around two of the smaller girls, entirely unaware of her older sister's presence. Lambkin, meanwhile, was nowhere to be seen.

"I should get my sister," Caroline said, feeling bad that her littlest sister might be missing out.

But Luke gave her hand a squeeze. "She'll come out of her own accord, or one of the others will get her." He smiled at her. "Just stay with me a while."

And though she knew she ought to concentrate on Lambkin, Luke's hand felt so very nice holding hers. And the day was one of the most beautiful summer Sundays she could remember, even before her world was turned upside down. The children were happy, there was joy in the air, and her own heart swelled with contentment. Perhaps, just once, she could wait a moment or two before hurrying off to tend to someone else.

"Very well," she said shyly. "But only for a few minutes."

Standing like that, on the periphery of the entertainment, the two of them watched the remarkably violent puppets together. Their laughter mingled with the cheers of the children, a comforting, comfortable silence existing between them as she leaned into him, and he brushed his thumb gently against her skin as he kept hold of her hand.

"I meant to tell you," Luke said after a short while. "I've thought of a solution to our Fox problem. It's why I came to find you."

She peered up at him, frowning. "You did?"

He nodded, but before he could begin to tell her what that solution might be, a carriage rattled into the square. A familiar carriage, pulled by two majestic draught horses, that Caroline had not seen for a week.

The driver paid no attention to the children and mothers who continued to flock onto the 'Green' to see the puppets, forcing many of them to dive out of the way or to be snatched out of the carriage's path at the last moment. The sight of it struck an old fear into Caroline's heart, her mind swarming with the memory of a winter almost four years ago. The thud of unseen hooves in the midst of the blizzard. Blood on the snow. Her father's scattered paintbrushes.

"Speak of the devil," Luke muttered, his eyes narrowing as the carriage came all the way around the square and pulled to a halt in front of Fox House.

The door opened and Mr. Fox got out, ignoring the pair as he breezed into his corrupt orphanage. Yet, there was something about his manner—a smugness greater than usual—that set alarm bells clanging in Caroline's head.

"I need to speak with him," she said, pulling her hand out of Luke's.

"I don't think that's wise," Luke tried to say, but Caroline was already hurrying inside, pursuing Mr. Fox down the too-warm hallways to his study.

He took out a key and slotted it into the lock, glancing back over his shoulder as he opened the door. "Ah, Miss Caroline, there you are. You have saved me the bother of summoning you. Please, do come in."

He stepped through and Caroline went after him, coming to a sharp standstill as she realised there was already someone in the study. Someone who should not have been there. Someone who should have been safely in the nursery with Rosemary, or playing with the other children. Indeed, Caroline was horrified with herself for not noticing that her littlest sister had been absent, wondering how she could have missed such a thing.

She was definitely at breakfast, but Mr. Fox wasn't here... was he? Did I miss him coming in?

"Lambkin, come to me," Caroline said, stretching out her hand. "Now."

The little girl sat quite happily upon Mr. Fox's high-backed chair, oblivious to the fact that she was in danger. She did not seem perturbed at all. Maybe, she had not realised that she had been locked in.

"Stay where you are," Mr. Fox commanded, wagging a finger.

Lambkin looked at him with a small frown but, to Caroline's dismay, she obeyed.

"What are you doing?" Caroline turned her fear on Mr. Fox, the words coming out as a hiss.

Mr. Fox partially closed the drapes, fending off the brightness of the summer sunlight that pierced the windows. "I have come to bring good tidings, Miss Caroline. A favour, if you will." He smiled, and she did not trust it one bit. "Naturally, I knew you would not be able to pay for Lambkin's care, and I figured you would not want anything bad to befall her. As such, I have made alternative arrangements."

"What sort of arrangements?" Caroline shot back, her heart pounding wildly. "I never said I would not be able to pay for Lambkin's care. I *can* and I will."

Mr. Fox tutted under his breath. "At great cost to yourself and your dignity, Miss Caroline. I could not have that, either." He sighed as if *she* was the troublesome one. "I have received an expression of interest from a couple that I know —well-to-do, excellent prospects, deeply in love with one another, but, tragically, unable to have children of their own."

"You can't..." Caroline rasped, understanding immediately.

"I can and I am," Mr. Fox replied with a dismissive wave of his hand. "I mean to accept their request to adopt her. She will be raised well, wanting for nothing."

"Mr. Fox, no," Caroline urged, her hands clasped. "Please, don't do this."

He smiled, as though he had hoped she might start to beg. "Of course, if *you* want to keep her and see her taken care of, then we could always return to that offer I mentioned?" He paused, tracing his fingertips across the edge of his desk. "You are very beautiful, Caroline, and so diligent with the children. An asset, certainly. And now that I know that what you said was true about where you earned your coin, then... perhaps it would not be so outlandish for us to marry. I would gladly raise your sisters as my own daughters, and lavish my attention on you, as my wife. Now that I know you are not impure, you understand."

Desperation clawed its way up from Caroline's innards, forcing her to step forwards, closer to her little sister. "Lambkin, please come to me."

"Stay where you are," Mr. Fox snapped, the little girl recoiling, shrinking into the high-backed chair. "There are two choices here, Caroline: you marry me, or you let this couple adopt Lambkin. There is no third or fourth choice. Well, there *is* a third choice, but you will not like it— Lambkin will end up where the rest end up, when their family cannot pay anymore."

All of the air rushed out of Caroline's lungs as she stood there, panting hard, gazing desperately at her little sister. If Lambkin was anyone else, that third choice would mean being taken to a real orphanage or the doorstep of a church, where Caroline could easily collect her later. But Caroline had the awful feeling that Mr. Fox would see to Lambkin's despatch personally, if she made that decision.

I can't marry him. I can't do it. But nor can I let my sister be taken away by strangers. Oh... what do I do? What do I do?

"I *can* pay, Mr. Fox," she pleaded. "Whatever it costs, I will pay. I will find a way, as I have always done."

He shook his head. "That is no longer a possibility, Caroline. I assumed that was obvious, but perhaps not." He expelled a weary breath. "So, I shall repeat myself: you marry me, you send Lambkin away, or you agree that her time here has ended, and she will leave in a different fashion."

"Mr. Fox, please," she begged. "Please, don't do this. I will do anything."

He smirked. "Apparently not." His expression darkened. "Do you know how fortunate you would be, to be married to me? Do you think I make this offer lightly? I will not repeat it if you leave this room, refusing me."

"I'll help her to pay whatever it costs to keep Lambkin here," Luke's voice interjected, his welcome figure stepping into the study. "She's not marrying you, Mr. Fox. I won't let you blackmail her into it. And I won't let you harm Lambkin or put her in harm's way."

Mr. Fox grinned from ear to ear, applauding slowly as Luke moved forward to take Caroline's hand.

"I did wonder if you would be joining us," the older man said, his eyes half-mad, "or if you would just be lurking somewhere nearby, as always."

"I promised to protect her," Luke growled, squeezing her hand.

Mr. Fox tilted his head to one side. "Did you now? That *is* surprising." He paused, smirking at Caroline. "Then again, I suppose you did not promise to protect her father, did you? Perhaps, you are more like your father than I thought—getting rid of the opposition, so to speak. I mean, *her* father certainly would not have accepted *you* as a prospect. Because of what you did, I guess you do not have to worry about that."

"What?" Caroline wheezed, her mind buzzing as though a nest of wasps had enveloped her skull.

"Don't," Luke warned Mr. Fox, though his hand trembled slightly in Caroline's.

Mr. Fox chuckled. "He did not tell you, Caroline, did he?"

"Tell me what?" she choked, her head spinning.

"Why, my dear," Mr. Fox replied with that awful grin, "that he was involved in your father's death."

CHAPTER 20

"Your beloved Luke was sent here by my dear cousin because he was witness to a crime," Mr. Fox explained, his tone so jarringly delighted that Caroline could barely listen. "A murder, to be exact. Of course, the poor boy could not behave himself, could not keep secrets—not back then, at least—and had been threatening to go to the constables with what he knew. So, my cousin had him brought to me, knowing I would never allow him to breathe a word."

Luke held tighter to Caroline's hand, bringing his hand up to her cheek, trying to get her to look at him. "I knew it was wrong to stay silent, Caro. I *wanted* to say something, but Mr. Fox and Quentin both threatened to blame me for what happened if I spoke up. I have no power, no influence, Caro—I couldn't do the right thing. They stopped me."

"Yet, you did not deem it appropriate to tell Caroline *herself* what you had seen," Mr. Fox pointed out, as Caroline struggled to stay standing, her head swimming.

She dug her fingernails into the palm of her free hand,

huffing out a strained breath as she rasped, "What happened? What did... Quentin do?"

"Oh, he saw an opportunity, that is all," Mr. Fox replied, so casually that it made Caroline want to take one of his paperweights and strike him across the temple with it. "He decided he could not be without that mother of yours, so he... 'created' an accident. He waited for your father, and he ran him down."

Caroline's eyes scrunched shut, her chest so tight she could not take a breath, her heart splintering as she thought of that day—not a tragic, terrible accident after all, but something that Quentin had planned. That despicable man had taken her father away from them, poisoned her mother's mind with that wretched medicine, and sold the three sisters off as if they were cattle at the market. That man had ruined all of their lives out of greed and jealousy, coveting what was not his.

"*You* were not supposed to be there, but once my cousin realised you had seen nothing, he continued with his plan," Mr. Fox proceeded in that same, gleeful tone. "And now, he has exactly what he always wanted, and no one would believe either of you if you spoke a word of it, so perhaps we ought to return to the matter at hand. Why, if you marry me, I could have Luke turned into the constables for you. Some justice—call it a wedding gift."

Wrenching her hand out of Luke's, she staggered backwards, breathing hard but drawing in no air at all. In that moment, her legs gave way, the shock of what she had heard knocking her off her feet. She crashed to the floor as darkness descended, though not even the oblivion of unconsciousness would be able to wash away what she now knew: about Quentin, about her father, about Luke, and the knotted web that connected them all.

As she fainted, she thought she had returned to that awful day for a moment, as she heard Luke's voice whispering, "I'm sorry. I'm so sorry."

You were the one who helped me to my feet that day. You knew, all this time. It was you...

* * *

Caroline jolted awake, her skin cold and clammy, her heart racing, fearing she might somehow find herself lying on that snowy street again. Someone was holding her, murmuring to her in a faraway voice, like she was submerged in bathwater.

"Caro?" The voice became clearer.

"Get away from me," she croaked, scrabbling to be free of Luke's embrace. "Don't you dare touch me!"

He released her as if her skin were white-hot, shrinking backwards with his hands up in a gesture of surrender. "Caro, if you would just let me explain, I—"

"I've heard more than enough," she hissed, tears pricking at her eyes. "You were there. You were with Quentin when he..." She could not finish the sentence, the old scars of three-and-a-half years ago cracking open afresh, the salt of the awful truth liberally poured into the wounds.

"I didn't know what he was planning, I swear it," Luke said desperately. "And when it happened, all I saw was you falling. I jumped right out of the carriage to help you. I didn't realise your father was struck until after. Quentin dragged me away from you, or I'd have stayed. I'd have stayed and told the constables everything."

She glared at him as a few tears spilled. "You had plenty of time to tell the truth. If not to the constables, then to me." Her voice hitched. "You tricked me, Luke. You... made yourself dear to me, knowing *that* secret."

"I tried to tell you a thousand times," he murmured, his eyes glimmering with sorrow. "Do you remember when I said I would help you because I owed you?"

Disgust wrenched at her stomach, hollowing her out. "*That* was the reason why?"

"Yes, but that's also when I almost told you," he replied, fumbling through his words. "I never wanted to keep it from you. But you heard Mr. Fox—he planned to pin it on me if I said a word. And he would do it, too."

She shook her head, refusing to listen. "You have had two years to tell me. There should have been no 'almost.' You *should* have told me."

"I know." He hung his head. "I know, but I didn't know how, and then so much time passed, and—"

"Where is she?" Caroline lumbered to her feet, panicked eyes darting this way and that. But she was alone in the study with Luke. Mr. Fox and, more importantly, Lambkin, were nowhere to be seen.

"Who?"

"Lambkin. Where is she?"

Luke frowned. "Mr. Fox sent her out of the room when you collapsed. Told her to go and play with the other children."

"No... No, no, no!" Caroline ran from the study, though her legs had not quite woken up yet.

She hurtled down the hallway and out of the front door, sprinting across the square until she reached the theatrical troupe. They had put away the puppets and were now teaching some kind of dance to the crowd of children, accompanied by instruments.

But Caroline would not have noticed if the performers

were standing on their heads, juggling live chickens whilst they breathed fire—all she noticed was that Mr. Fox's carriage was gone, and Lambkin was not to be found amongst the children.

"Estie!" Caroline shouted, startling a few of the spectators.

Esther jumped up, wearing a puzzled frown as she walked to her older sister. "What's wrong? What are you shouting for?"

"Have you seen Lambkin? Is she out here somewhere?" Caroline asked, panic simmering in her voice.

Esther quirked an eyebrow. "She went with Abigail and Olivia."

A tiny flame of hope flickered in Caroline's chest, for Abigail and Olivia were two of Lambkin's friends. Abigail was four and Olivia was five, and the three girls always slept side-by-side on a cot in the back room of the nursery, where the infants stayed until they were old enough to work at the mill. If Lambkin was with them, then perhaps she really had just been sent to play with the other children.

"Where are they?" Caroline asked, a note more calmly.

Esther shrugged. "Mr. Fox took them to the sweet shop. We were all terribly jealous."

Caroline froze, her dread a tonne weight, sinking into the pit of her stomach. "He took the girls in the carriage?"

"Of course. Mr. Fox would not *walk* to the sweet shop," Esther replied with a nervous smile, her tone too bright. "Caro, what's wrong?"

Caroline could not speak, a cold sweat prickling down the back of her neck. Mr. Fox was not generous unless it benefited him; he would not simply take three of the girls to the sweet shop for the sake of it. Indeed, she did not believe there was a sweet shop involved at all, but rather adoptive parents, ready and waiting to take away 'unwanted' children.

"I'll go," Luke's soft voice interjected, his hand tentatively resting on Caroline's shoulder. "I'll search every last sweet shop, and the mill too. I won't stop until I know where he has taken her. You stay here and pack anything you have. I'll bring her back; I don't care what it costs me. And when I do, you have to be ready to leave at once. Both of you."

Caroline could not reply to him. She could hardly bear the sight of him, or the touch of his hand on her shoulder. Nevertheless, she watched as he took off, running across the square and disappearing down one of the narrow streets that branched off.

He had said he would help her; he had said that he owed her, and if ever there was a moment where she had to set aside her anger and let him do what she could not, it was now. He knew the city better than she did; he knew Mr. Fox's haunts and hideaways, he knew of places she could not have guessed in a hundred years, whereas she would have been searching blindly. But that did not mean she would forgive him. Indeed, she did not think she had it in her to *ever* forgive him for his silence.

"Caro, what is happening?" Esther's voice trembled as she spoke.

"We are packing," Caroline replied, taking Esther by the hand. "As soon as Luke brings Lambkin back, we are departing with everything we have left, and we are returning to London without delay. And when we are there, we are going to get our mother back too, and we are going to make Quentin pay for what he has done."

She pulled Esther across the square, praying with all of her might that Luke would keep his promise. And when he did, she would leave him behind and never think of him again. *That* was the closest thing to forgiveness she would ever be able to offer the man she had accidentally fallen in love with. The man who had kissed her and broken her heart, all in the same day.

CHAPTER 21

It was two hours before news arrived, though it did not come from the source that Caroline had expected. Rather, it came in the form of two carriages—one belonging to Mr. Fox, and one that was unfamiliar to her.

Caroline watched from the upstairs window where she had spent every moment since Luke left, biting her fingernails, chewing her lip, pacing back and forth, willing Lambkin to be returned to her. It had not taken her long to pack the few belongings she owned, and the same was true for Esther, who stood at her sister's side at the window.

"She's safe," Esther whispered, expelling a relieved breath. "Look—she's there, and so are Abigail and Olivia!"

Caroline narrowed her eyes, observing the trio of little girls who had stepped out of the carriage ahead of Mr. Fox. They were sharing what appeared to be a paper bag of sweets between them, but Caroline was not fooled. Something else was afoot. Something pertaining to that second carriage that had just come to a standstill.

"I told you they had just gone to the sweet shop," Esther

said with a smile, which faded when she looked at her sister's face.

Caroline had told her younger sister *some* of the truth, explaining that Mr. Fox was threatening to have Lambkin adopted, but she had held back the revelation that Quentin had killed their father, and that Luke had been a witness to it. Esther did not need to feel the pain of those old wounds reopening, whether it made Caroline a hypocrite or not.

"It was a trick," Caroline muttered. "It's always a trick with Mr. Fox."

Just then, the door to the second carriage opened, and a handsome young gentleman in fine clothing held out his hand to help an extraordinarily beautiful young woman down the step to the ground. He pressed a kiss to her cheek, both of them smiling as they followed Mr. Fox into Fox House.

"Stay here," Caroline instructed. "When I tell you to leave, we are leaving."

"No," Esther replied stubbornly. "I'm coming with you."

Caroline had no time to argue, hurrying across the landing and down the stairs, hoping to cut the couple and Mr. Fox off before they could reach wherever they were headed. But they were quicker than she had expected, and by the time she had caught up, she was half-stumbling into Mr. Fox's study.

Abigail and Olivia had vanished somewhere along the way, but Lambkin was there... held in the arms of the beautiful young woman. To make matters worse, Lambkin was laughing and playing with the lady's hair, offering her sweets from the paper bag. And that exquisitely pretty lady was gazing back at Lambkin as if she was the most wonderful child she had ever seen.

"Ah, Miss Caroline, Miss Esther, what excellent timing!"

Mr. Fox cried, clapping his hands together. "I was about to summon the two of you, as Mr. and Mrs. Hyles thought it would be of merit to have you here, and to meet you."

The young lady—Mrs. Hyles, presumably—flashed a pearly white smile at Caroline. "You must be the sisters I have heard so much about? Oh, it is wonderful to meet you both. There is so much I want to ask you about this darling girl. I hear that she has recently turned three, is that right? Was your mother fair-haired? The little one has such lovely blonde—"

"Don't speak of my mother in the past tense," Caroline interrupted harshly. "My sister *has* a mother, alive and well. She is not for sale. You cannot have her."

Mrs. Hyles frowned at her husband, who canted his head, wearing a similar expression of confusion.

"We were under the assumption that the three of you were orphans," Mr. Hyles said, with a stern look at Mr. Fox.

"Well, you were misinformed," Caroline shot back.

Mr. Fox put on a tight smile and stepped in. "Whilst these three sisters *do* have a mother living, *this* particular child was not registered, and I have a written declaration that the mother wants nothing to do with her." He went to his desk and drew out a letter, passing it to the Hyles' with an air of false apology. "I wrote to her with some urgency when the money for dear Lambkin's care was not paid, and this is what I received. Since then, I have been taking care of Lambkin out of the goodness of my heart, whilst searching for the right people to adopt her as their own."

"How dare you," Caroline snarled. "*I* have paid for her care. You have never done anything out of the goodness of your heart in all your life, I would imagine. You are *lying* to these people!"

Mr. Hyles read the letter whilst Mrs. Hyles concentrated

on Lambkin, bouncing the little girl on her hip, smiling at her adoringly.

Mr. Fox cleared his throat. "I do apologise for Miss Caroline. It is an emotional moment for these two sisters, as I am sure you can appreciate. They were not to know that their mother had rescinded all responsibility over their youngest sister. But, as you can see, it is all there."

"If that is signed by my mother, it was done under duress or a lack of awareness," Caroline retorted. "She will not have known what she was signing because she cannot read or write—she is illiterate, and I would stake all I own on her husband weaving untruths, writing that 'on her behalf' for his own benefit."

Mrs. Hyles furrowed her brow, her eyes filled with dismay. "Oh goodness, I do hope that is not true. I have been so excited to take Lambkin home with us, to cherish her and adore her, but... if the mother *does* want her, I could not take her. It would not be right, though I shall be so very sorry."

Caroline allowed herself a tiny breath of relief, for she had not expected the couple that Mr. Fox had spoken of to be so reasonable. The lady, certainly, though the gentleman continued to inspect the letter.

Just then, Caroline felt a light tug on her sleeve and glanced down to find Esther gazing at Lambkin and Mrs. Hyles. Not with outrage or disapproval, but with a sad sort of warmth, of hope.

"We should agree, Caro," Esther whispered.

Caroline gaped at her sister. "Have you taken leave of your senses? That is our *sister*. I will not agree."

"But... think of the life she might have," Esther replied in a hushed tone, still staring. "Think of the life she would have with us, wherever we end up, and then consider this alternative. Quentin will never let us stay in London with Mama. Quentin will never let us have our mother back. We might very well find ourselves on the street or at a workhouse, struggling to survive. I don't mind that for myself, as long as I'm with you, but... Lambkin has an opportunity here. We shouldn't be... selfish, Caro."

Caroline could not believe what she was hearing. Ever since Lambkin was born, they had all stuck together—three sisters, facing whatever came their way together. How could Esther even *think* of letting these strangers take Lambkin away?

"I realise you do not know us," Mrs. Hyles said softly, her blue eyes friendly and warm. "I realise this is difficult for you, but I promise you, on everything that I hold dear, that I will love this little girl as if she has always been my own. She will want for nothing. She will have her own bedchamber, all the toys she could desire, an excellent education; she will never go hungry, she will never know hardship and, of course, you would be welcome to see her whenever you please. We do not live far. By Woodhouse Moor, just opposite where they are building the new grammar school. Our is the house with the two stags by the gate."

Hesitation held Caroline rigid, her gaze flitting between Mrs. Hyles, Lambkin, and Mr. Fox. Was Esther right? Was this an opportunity that Lambkin could not miss? Was it selfish to want to keep the trio together, when their future was so uncertain?

"I believe her," Esther whispered.

But Caroline could not decide, utterly torn; it was too great a choice to make.

However, as she met Mr. Fox's eyes and marked his leering face, the scales began to tip in one direction more than the other. Evidently, he was expecting her to refuse the adoption and accept *his* offer instead of letting Lambkin go with the pleasant couple. Had the couple not been so nice, had Esther not made her think twice, maybe she would have given in at last.

"Do you swear to me that you will raise my little sister with the same love that she would have received from us?" Caroline asked, her heart already cracking.

Mrs. Hyles nodded effusively. "I swear it, Caroline."

"As do I, Miss," Mr. Hyles added with a shy smile. "This will make my wife happier than anything in the world, and it would be my honour to cherish this dear little girl as her father. I promise, she will have a wonderful life with us and, as my wife said, you are welcome to visit whenever you please."

Esther took hold of Caroline's hand and squeezed it gently, whispering, "Let her go with them, Caro. It is the best chance she has."

"Very well," Caroline said, closing her eyes as if that would make it any easier. "Very well, you can... take her. But we *will* be visiting her, and if you don't keep your promise to me, I will take her back."

Her heart shattered, even as she said what had to be said. Esther *was* right; this was Lambkin's best and only chance to escape a life of hardship and uncertainty. She would have the sort of life that Caroline and Esther had enjoyed until their father was killed, the sort of life that she had never been allowed to experience because of that. Caroline could not be selfish, even if it hurt unbearably.

"Oh, thank you!" Mrs. Hyles rushed forwards to embrace the two older sisters, tears welling in her big blue eyes. "Thank you, with all of my heart. I shall not disappoint you; I promise faithfully, here and now. Thank you."

Caroline did not hug the woman in return, concentrating on Lambkin, who clearly did not know what on earth was going on. The little girl put her small arms around Caroline's neck, and Caroline held her in return, pressing a tender kiss to Lambkin's brow.

"I will miss you so very much," she murmured, her voice thick with pain. "But we will see you soon, and we will always be nearby. I love you, sweet girl. I love you."

Lambkin grinned. "I love you!"

"Eat all of the delicious things," Esther chimed in, joining the embrace. "Play with all of the toys, enjoy your education as much as you can, and do not miss us too much, though we will miss you. We love you, dearest Lambkin. Make us incredibly jealous, won't you?"

Lambkin chuckled and kissed each of her sisters. "I love you! Can we have sweets now?"

"You can have the rest of them in the carriage," Mrs. Hyles said with a fond smile.

Lambkin seemed to consider the suggestion and nodded amenably. "Let's go to carriage. I have my sweets."

Whether or not the intention had been for the Hyles' to take Lambkin there and then, Caroline did not know, but it seemed fruitless to delay the inevitable. The Hyles' seemed to think the same thing as, with many thanks and farewells and promises, the husband and wife left Mr. Fox's study with Lambkin in their arms and in their possession.

Caroline and Esther followed them all the way to the front door, and came out to wave Lambkin off as the new family disappeared inside the carriage. The little girl, too focussed on her sweets, did not even look back as the carriage pulled away from the pavement and did a round of the square, before turning off towards what Caroline hoped would be a new and exciting future.

"I can't bear this," she mumbled, plucking out her handkerchief to dab away her tears. "I always thought I would be able to keep her with us."

Esther nodded, wiping her eyes on the corner of her apron. "I know, but I really think it's for the best. You did all you could, Caro. That will always mean something to her."

"I hope so," Caroline said with a heavy sigh.

As she stood there, watching the spot where Lambkin had disappeared, a flurry of fresh anger replaced her regret. Of course, she was aware that she could never have offered Lambkin a luxurious life, but she *knew* that she would have been able to keep Lambkin with her, living a decent life, if it had not been for the spiteful actions of one man.

Without a word, she spun around and marched back inside, storming down the hallway with a thundercloud hanging over her head, ready to strike lightning upon that wretched beast.

But the moment Caroline strode into Mr. Fox's study, she could not see him anywhere... not until she heard the door close with a thud behind her, and heard the turn of a key in the lock.

CHAPTER 22

"I suppose you think yourself extremely clever," Mr. Fox spat, his blue eyes glinting with a fury that Caroline had not seen from him before.

She darted to the other side of the room, putting as much distance between them as possible. "Isn't that what you wanted? Why would you go to the trouble of finding a nice couple to adopt Lambkin if you didn't want her to be adopted?"

"You are no fool, Caroline." He slipped the key into his pocket and stood staring at her, the air so thick and hot in the study that it cloyed in Caroline's throat. "Although, you are weaker than I thought you were. Where was your determination? Where was your insistence that you would do anything to keep your sister with you?"

Caroline swallowed tightly. "I realised that what they could give her was something I couldn't."

And it hurts so very much—a pain greater than anything you could inflict upon me.

She jumped as a loud bang erupted through the room.

Mr. Fox twisted his head back to glare at the door, where another bang sounded... and another and another, followed by the unmistakable sound of Esther's distress.

"Open this door!" the younger girl howled. "Open it right now, Mr. Fox!"

A moment later, Rosemary's voice and fists joined in. "Mr. Fox, you turn that girl out of there at once! Don't you lay a hand on her! I don't care if it costs me my employment—you let her go!"

The pummelling on the door became a barrage that sounded like far more than two people, but the door was crafted from thick hardwood, the lock sturdy and unrelenting. No one could get out, and no one could get in, not without the key in Mr. Fox's pocket.

"I am not a monster, Caroline," he said in a silky, unsettling tone. "I *will* let you leave, just as soon as you consent to be my wife. Failing that, as soon as you have accepted that you will bear my child, no matter how long it takes."

Caroline backed up until she could not retreat any further, her spine pressed flat to the red brick wall. Her panicked eyes searched the study for anything she might use as a weapon, settling on the paperweight that she had considered bludgeoning him with before.

She lunged for it, raising it up. "If you don't let me leave of my own accord, I won't hesitate."

"To what?" He laughed coldly. "You do not have the strength to overwhelm me, Caroline, regardless of what you might have in your hand. Even if it were a pistol, you would not be able to fire it before I had reached you and taken it from you."

Her hand trembled, her palm so clammy that the smooth paperweight threatened to slip from her grasp. "I do *not* accept either of your proposals. And now that Lambkin is safe, you have no hold over me anymore."

"On the contrary." He stalked towards her. "You still have one other sister, remember? I believe she is the one trying to break down my door."

"She's more likely to kill you than I am," Caroline shot back, raising up the paperweight, struggling to hold her nerve with every step Mr. Fox took towards her.

All the while, Esther and Rosemary continued to thump on the door, yelling and shouting for help.

In a flash, Mr. Fox sprinted around the desk to grab at Caroline. Unleashing a yelp of terror, she managed to move her shaky legs, stumbling around to the opposite side of the desk. She knew she had to keep that mahogany between them, or he *would* catch her, and she did not want him to have the satisfaction of taking what he wanted from her.

Like predator and prey, they circled the desk, Caroline so intently focussed on him that her eyes began to blur. Meanwhile, the drumming of fists on the door matched the frantic beat of her heart. They were not going to make it inside; no one was coming to help her and, deep down, she knew that this chase was just delaying the inevitable. What was worse, Mr. Fox seemed to be enjoying himself.

"Shall we do this all day?" he asked with a smile. "You will tire before me."

"I wouldn't be so sure about that. I have more to lose," she retorted, readjusting her grip on the paperweight.

He laughed and, just as she reached the point where the high-backed chair narrowed the channel around the back of the desk, he made his move. He shot forwards so fast that she had barely any time to react, and though she tried to turn and run, his hand snatched a fistful of her dress.

She screamed as he yanked her backwards, his arm snaking around her waist, pulling her to him.

"That was fine entertainment," he whispered in her ear, "but I am weary of your games."

She shuddered as his wet lips pressed against her cheek, and kicked backwards as hard as she could, catching him in the shin. He roared in pain but his arm around her waist did not loosen; it tightened, the strength in his fury constricting her, threatening to crush her ribs.

Just as she feared that the worst was about to happen, and her fight was over, an almighty series of bangs thudded on the study door, louder than before. A moment later, it exploded inward; a stream of figures in dark cloaks pouring into the room, with one familiar face at the head of the group, leading them inside.

"Him! He's the one!" Luke cried, jabbing a finger in Mr. Fox's direction. "He's the one that's been killing children, stealing children, concealing murders, and breaking the laws of child labour!"

Mr. Fox staggered away from Caroline, his eyes wild, his mouth agape in disbelief as the constables swarmed him. "Nonsense!" he shouted. "That boy is lying! I would never do such things. I am a respectable gentleman and businessman. I—"

"We saw your mill, Mr. Fox," one of the constables interrupted with a scowl. "We've seen your ledgers. We've seen what you do. In truth, we've been after you for a while, watching and waiting, but we never had the evidence to arrest you."

"Until now," Luke said, panting hard as if he had run there.

The constables surrounded Mr. Fox, seizing him roughly. He attempted to fight back, but there were too many, and he was cornered. Caroline watched as they dragged him away, though there was little satisfaction; she would not breathe easily until he was in prison.

Why could you not have come a little sooner? Her heart ached, for if the constables *had*, then Lambkin would not have been taken away by the Hyles'. Would they give her back now? Was there any point, when the fact remained that Caroline and Esther could not give Lambkin the life she deserved?

Unless... A thought came to her: a way to restore everything to the way it had been, and to put the broken family back together.

"There are women in the room past the kitchens who are involved," Rosemary hurriedly told the constables.

One of them nodded to her, then to his fellow men. "They'll start fleeing. Catch 'em and put 'em on the cart. Whether they're guilt of something or not, they'll be willing to speak against Mr. Fox. Don't let any get away."

The constables took off, their footsteps echoing down the hallway, the chaos settling into a strange quiet inside the study. Caroline braced her hands against the desk to catch her breath, whilst Luke approached cautiously.

"I showed them everything," he said, coming to a standstill on the other side of the desk. "I... thought it would help get Lambkin back quicker than if I searched for her."

Caroline raised her gaze. "Lambkin is gone. Adopted."

"What?" His eyebrows shot up. "Where? We have to go and fetch her. Come on, we'll leave now."

He tried to reach for her hand, but she withdrew, shaking her head.

"They are good people. She'll have a better life." Her voice cracked. "There's no reason to fetch her back anymore. It would be selfish, in truth, to snatch that hope, that chance, away from her."

Luke stared at her as if she were mad, disbelief etched across his handsome face. No small amount of heartbreak, too, for he had adored Lambkin. He had spoiled her, cherished her, and helped to raise her, keeping his promises. That was not to be disregarded, but still—he had kept such a terrible secret from Caroline. A secret she could not begin to forgive.

"I'm sorry, Caro," he murmured, coming closer.

She did not back away as he came around to her side of the desk, but she straightened up, staring at him with a stony gaze.

"I'm so very sorry for not telling you the truth when I had the chance," he continued, his voice thick. "It was cowardly. I thought you would hate me, and I didn't want you to hate me. I should've known you'd hate me even more if I *didn't* say a word."

He stepped forwards to embrace her, clearly mistaking her lack of evasion. Shaking her head, she shoved him in the chest, determined to keep him at arm's length so that he could not convince her or persuade her by reminding her of happier times.

"We lost everything because Quentin—and, by association, you—killed my father. I realise that you weren't holding the reins, and you probably *didn't* know what was planned, but I won't forgive you for staying silent," she told him icily. "I won't forgive you for letting Quentin trap my mother to save your own skin. If you'd told me, I could have changed things, and we might not be here now. You took that opportunity from me, and that's what I can't forgive, so don't ask me to."

She retreated from him, crossing the study and stepping

out into the hallway as chaos continued to reign throughout Fox House. Constables were dragging the 'Mothers' out into the square, whilst they protested their innocence or yelled that Mr. Fox had forced them to agree, observed by the residents who were still out on the 'Green,' enjoying the last of the day's warmth.

Mr. Fox himself sat in the cart with his head down, making himself as unnoticeable as possible. An echo of the way that Caroline and her sisters had come to Fox House in the first place. Fitting, but still not quite satisfying.

"It mightn't come to anything," Rosemary said, appearing on the step behind Caroline. Esther beside her. "You know Mr. Fox is wily as they come, but Luke did a fine thing, fetching those constables. I daresay he saved your life, Caro."

Caroline took a shaky breath. "Yes, I daresay he did."

Twice now, she realised with some conflict. *More than twice, if I'm being honest... but all out of guilt.*

"What do we do now?" Esther asked, slipping her hand into Caroline's.

Rosemary sighed. "You've a place here. That hasn't changed. You have more of a place now, so long as Mr. Fox stays where he belongs, in the darkest prison cell they can find."

"Maybe one day we'll come back," Caroline said, almost to herself. "But there's something I have to do first. Something you can help me with, Estie, if you want to, though I won't blame you if you want to stay here."

Esther peered up at her. "I already told you that I'm sticking with you. So, what do we have to do?"

The sisters might not have been able to keep Lambkin with them, but there was one person who could get her back and make it worthwhile; one person who might be encouraged if she found out that Quentin killed her beloved husband; one person who needed saving first, before they could hope to retrieve Lambkin.

"Estie," Caroline said with a breath. "We're going back to London."

CHAPTER 23

The journey back to London was longer than the journey had been to reach Leeds, those years ago. Yet, it was not weighted with the terror that had pursued the sisters up to Yorkshire. They were not bound and afraid for their lives, jostled around in the back of a cart. They could take their time, seeing more of the countryside that they had missed the first time around, relishing the fine weather and the kindness of strangers.

The sisters had slept wherever they could: hay barns, out in the fields beneath pristine starlight, beneath sprawling oak trees where they were awoken by the dropped acorns of angry squirrels, and on two occasions, in the homes of those kindly strangers who had willingly offered up shelter and food to the two girls, asking nothing in return.

As for their transportation, Rosemary had given Caroline enough money to pay for the stagecoaches that would take them to the Capital. Although, in her heart, Caroline suspected that the money had come from a different source.

"I've had it tucked away for a day such as this for years," Rosemary had insisted, but the old woman had never been a particularly good liar. Her 'tell' was not being able to look someone in the eyes when she was fibbing, and she had not been able to meet Caroline's gaze once.

"I think I can see it!" Esther said eagerly, her face pressed to the pane of the stagecoach window.

The man selling tickets for the stagecoach in the last town they had stopped at had assured the two sisters that it would take them directly to London, but Caroline was not in the habit of trusting men anymore. As such, she had decided that she would not believe they were going to reach London until she saw Covent Garden again. More specifically, the window of her father's studio.

"I *can*, Caro!" Esther insisted. "We are almost there!"

Closing her eyes, Caroline mustered a smile. "Let me know when you see St. Paul's Cathedral."

As she sat there, trying to quieten her mind, a frown creased her brow. She could not explain it, but an uneasiness had followed her from Leeds—not that initial terror she had felt after being sold by Quentin, but a feeling like she was missing something. For the past few days, it had caught her unawares, whilst she was eating delicious stew with Esther or curled up on blankets under the stars: a strange feeling like they were not quite alone.

Is it because of Lambkin? She rubbed her temples with her fingertips, like that might nudge an explanation to the forefront of her mind. *It could be, but... I don't know.*

She cracked open one eye and peered discreetly around at the other passengers in the stagecoach: an elderly couple sharing a slice of pie; a mother and a sleeping baby; two young gentlemen; and a slightly older woman, perhaps forty, travelling alone. None were familiar to her, none had been on any of the other stagecoaches, and yet Caroline wondered if, maybe, there was a spy in their midst.

Has Mr. Fox sent someone after us? Are they biding their time? What if they run on ahead and let Quentin know we're coming? It *was* that sort of feeling: a prickle up the back of her neck. And the closer to London they got, the more it became a burn, robbing her of the peace she had almost achieved over the past few days.

That's ridiculous, she told herself a moment later. *He had no time to do such a thing. He didn't know the constables were coming.*

Yet, the feeling persisted.

As such, when the stagecoach finally came to a halt in the piazza of Covent Garden, she did not pause to stare at the window that had once belonged to her father's studio. She grabbed Esther by the hand, retrieved their paltry luggage, and dragged her towards Mayfair as fast as their respective legs would carry them. There was no time for reminiscing, and even less time for Caroline to wallow in the sorrow of what had actually befallen her father—a fate far worse than the story of an unfortunate accident that she had believed until so very recently.

"What if he doesn't live here anymore?" Esther asked, wiser than her years, as the sisters slowed to a breathless walk on the gleaming, pretty streets of Mayfair.

The square of private park that Caroline had longed to walk through, peering miserably from her chamber window, looked particularly beautiful in the late-afternoon sunlight; the grass almost golden, the trees rustling happily, whilst two spaniels chased each other around the sturdy trunks.

"Then we search London until we find him," Caroline replied, spotting the townhouse up ahead.

Her heart began to beat an uneven rhythm that made her stomach roil, cold sweat slicking her brow as she approached that awful place. It did not look as bright nor as inviting as the other townhouses, though they were all identical. There was a dullness, a greyness, a misery to Quentin's that could not be mistaken; he *had* to still be there, sucking the life out of her mother.

"Do we smack him senseless immediately, or do we wait?" Esther asked with a small smile.

Caroline managed a chuckle. "We wait until we have seen our mother, *then* we attack."

"A splendid plan." Esther weaved her arm through Caroline's, the two sisters reaching the porch steps of the townhouse.

They walked up together, but it was Caroline who took a steadying breath, then another, and rang the bell for admittance. She heard the jingle of the bells inside the house, remembering that awful sound: it had always meant another party where Heather would be paraded around as Mrs. Rawle, dressed in a garish gown, so consumed by the laudanum that she could not stand without assistance.

Footsteps approached and Caroline held her breath.

The door opened, a stern face peeking out through a conservative gap. "Yes?"

It was an old woman that Caroline did not recognise, wearing her greying hair in a dated style; two plaits looping around her ears, the rest scraped back into a low bun. She had sharp blue eyes, creased around the edges as if she were staring into the sun, and thin lips that were pressed into a grim line.

"We are here to see Mr. and Mrs. Rawle," Caroline said, as calmly as she could.

The woman sniffed. "Mr. Rawle isn't here at the moment."

"When will he return?" Caroline asked, a note too eagerly.

"That is none of your concern," the woman retorted.

Caroline saw the slam before it came and threw herself forwards, sliding her foot into the narrow gap and heaving with all her might to stop the woman from closing the door in her face. As stern as the woman looked, she was no match for Caroline's desperation. Nor Esther's; the younger woman barging the door with her shoulder, and a grunt of determination.

The old woman stumbled backwards with a gasp, the two sisters tumbling into the entrance hall that had not changed one bit since they were misled away.

"I shall send for the constables!" the woman, evidently the housekeeper or something of that ilk, cried out.

"You will do no such thing," Caroline shot back, catching her breath. "We are Mr. Rawle's stepdaughters. We have every right to be here, and if you send for the constables, that is precisely what we shall say. I have the documents to prove it, so all you will succeed in doing is making yourself look like a fool."

She did not, but the housekeeper did not need to know that.

This might have been easier if Luke were here. He could have held her whilst we searched, Caroline mused, hurriedly shoving the traitorous thought away. Luke did not speak up, Luke did not stop Quentin, Luke did not deserve a single moment of her contemplation.

"Stepdaughters?" The housekeeper narrowed her eyes. "The master doesn't have stepdaughters."

"We are Heather's daughters," Caroline said, her voice

colder than before. "By that reckoning, we are your master's stepdaughters, even if we would rather be anything else. If Mr. Rawle isn't here, where is *she*? Where is our mother?"

A flash of something like understanding crossed the housekeeper's face, and though the furrows in her brow did not lessen and her eyes were no warmer, she turned and pointed up the stairs. "She is in her bedchamber. She is always in her bedchamber." She paused. "She isn't well."

"No, I expect not, despite all of the 'medicine' that your *master* gives her," Caroline muttered, striding past the old woman and heading up the stairs with Esther right behind her.

On the way up, Esther whispered, "Do you think she'll actually send for the constables?"

"I hope she does, so they can grab Quentin when he comes home and put him in chains," Caroline replied, coming to the landing.

She had not forgotten the room where her mother had always languished, and headed directly for it, not giving the housekeeper a second thought.

But the bedchamber and the woman Caroline called 'Mama' *had* changed. Indeed, nothing could have prepared Caroline for what had become of her mother, as she ground to a halt just past the threshold, her hand flying to her mouth.

A skeleton lay curled up on dirty coverlets. A living skeleton that rasped and wheezed, lifting a gaunt face to stare at Caroline with listless eyes. A clawed hand weakly reached out, a whisper hissing through the stagnant air of the gloomy room—one word: "Medicine."

The curtains were drawn, tallow candles burning, the sour scent of sickness stinging Caroline's nostrils.

"Mama?" she croaked, noting the stringy strands of hair

that had once been glorious auburn waves; the pallid flesh that sagged from bone, the hollow cheeks and eyes, the cracked and bloodless lips. She could have curved her thumb and forefinger around her mother's wrist and still had room.

The woman frowned, her eyes glassy. "Medicine."

"No," Caroline said, her voice trembling. "You've had enough medicine, Mama. You'll never have another mouthful of that awful stuff again."

At that moment, Esther entered, her gasp ripping through the air. "Mama!"

Heather, or what was left of her, squinted. "I need... my medicine."

"Mama, it's us!" Esther cried. "We came back for you. Mama... it's us."

"She doesn't recognise us right now, but she will," Caroline said with all the confidence she could muster, refusing to let herself crumble.

It's just the laudanum. Once she stops taking it, she'll be our mother again. She has to. She clung to that as she approached the bed, wishing for a second time that Luke was with them. He would have been able to carry Heather out of that room with no trouble at all.

"We have to get her out of here," Caroline said, as she began to wrap the filthy blankets around her mother, ignoring the woman's pleas for medicine.

Together, Caroline and Esther managed to carry their mother out of the foetid bedchamber, clumsily wielding her down the hallway to the landing. Their mother weighed almost nothing at all, and they had gained some wiry strength from their time at the textile mill, yet they struggled, sweating and staggering their way to the top of the stairs.

"Where... are we going to take her?" Esther wheezed.

Caroline readjusted her grip on her mother's upper half. "To a physician."

"We have no money, Caro! No physician will take care of her."

"They will when they see her necklace," Caroline replied, pointing her chin towards the ostentatious ruby that hung limply around her mother's throat. She remembered it from one of the parties Quentin had hosted; it would be enough to pay for the talents of not just any sawbones, but a truly gifted doctor.

Esther frowned across at her sister. "Fine, that solves that. But how do we get her down the—"

The front door flew inwards, a blur of unbridled fury charging in. The housekeeper, it seemed, had not gone to fetch the constables, but she *had* gone to fetch someone else: the spider at the centre of this tangled, despicable web.

"Set my wife down!" Quentin roared, running for the stairs. "Leave this house and leave my wife alone! If you do not, I will send for the constables at once! I will send for all of Bow Street if I must!"

"I am counting on it," Caroline shouted, her words making Quentin stop dead, halfway up the stairs. "You send for them, send for all of them, so I can have a crowd when I tell them what you did to my father."

Quentin's hand curled around the banister, his knuckles whitening. "Not one of them would believe you."

"Not before, I agree, but they will now," Caroline replied, surprised by the cool calm of her voice. "Your *son* intends to testify against you for the murder of my father, and I would not be at all shocked if Mr. Fox does too. At present, I'm certain he would do anything to avoid a severe sentence for his crimes. He might well pin everything on you, claim that *you* are the secret architect behind the baby farm. Truly, there's no telling what depths he'll stoop to, to escape punishment."

Of course, she had no idea what Mr. Fox would do, or if he would mention Quentin at all… but the more afraid she could make the wretched man in front of her, the better. She needed him to be so terrified for his future that he would not even mutter a word of complaint as she and Esther left with their mother.

"He has been arrested," Caroline added for good measure, in case it was not obvious.

Quentin blanched, the whites of his eyes showing. "He said he would incriminate me?"

"He is *your* cousin. What do you think?"

His grip on the banister tightened, veins protruding through the top of his hand. "It was… it was an accident," he rasped, his throat bobbing. "Your father's death—it was an accident. I did not know he was in the road. There was a blizzard, for goodness' sake. I could not see anything."

"But you waited," Caroline said calmly.

A memory popped into her mind unbidden, of Quentin asking Caroline's father when he would next be at his studio so that he could come by. A friendly enough question, but there had been nothing friendly about Quentin's intention. She saw that now, cursing herself for missing it, cursing herself for not seeing through Quentin's façade when it mattered.

"You waited near to his studio, knowing your moment would come. You asked him, remember?" Her eyes hardened, her voice carrying an edge of threat that she had never heard from herself before. "I can't profess to know how long you were planning it, but I imagine the idea really began to form after you saw us that night by Sadler's Wells. Saw my mother, I should say."

Quentin quickly looked away, confirming her suspicions.

"It was no accident," Caroline continued. "Luke told me everything. Rather, Mr. Fox told me everything, and if he can tell me, he can tell the magistrates. *I* will tell the magistrates. Of course, we *could* come to an arrangement."

It was at that moment that she realised that Esther was looking at her strangely, her mouth agape, her eyes filling with tears. "What are you talking about?"

"I'm sorry, Estie." Caroline's mask of vengeance slipped for a moment. "I planned to tell you after we had rescued Mama. I found out the day the puppets came to the Green. There wasn't much time afterwards to explain everything, and I... couldn't find the words."

Esther flinched as if she had been nipped. "We've been travelling for days. You could have told me then."

"I know, but—"

Quentin lunged, barrelling up the stairs like some manner of unnatural creature, spewed out of the underworld. His nostrils flared, his eyes burning, and Caroline knew that he would not let her or her sister leave that house alive. She had not played her move quick enough, too distracted by the hypocritical secret she had kept from her sister. Indeed, she had intended to make Quentin an offer, but it was too late for that now.

Suddenly, Luke was there in the entrance hall, bounding up the stairs at a rapid pace, catching up to Quentin as he was about to strike at Caroline. Luke seized hold of the back of Quentin's tailcoat and pulled with all the strength in his powerful arms, wrenching Quentin away from the two girls and their mother.

But Luke must have pulled too hard, his balance not quite solid enough on the staircase. His eyes flew wide as he began to fall, still holding Quentin's tails in his gripped fists.

"Luke!" Caroline heard herself scream as he tumbled backwards.

Time quickened, the two men becoming a blur as they fell down the stairs together: a tangle of limbs and bones to be broken, rolling over and over one another, thudding all the way to the bottom.

And when they hit the tiles of the entrance hall, neither of them was moving.

CHAPTER 24

Setting her mother down on the landing, Caroline hurtled down the stairs as fast as her shaky legs would permit, praying all the while: *Let him be alive. Let him be alive. Please, I beg of you, let him be all right.*

She sank to her knees at Luke's side, shoving aside Quentin so she could pull Luke into her lap. With trembling hands, she touched his face, a ragged cut leaking blood above his right eye. She did not hesitate to whip out her handkerchief, pressing it to the wound, gazing down at his lovely face and his closed eyes, willing him to open them.

"Luke?" she urged. "Luke, please..."

This can't be happening. Please. Please, don't say that I've lost him. Please.

One eyelid cracked open slightly, a sad smile curving his lips. "I couldn't save... your father," he rasped, struggling for each word, "but I couldn't make... the same mistake twice."

"You shouldn't be here," she murmured, cradling his head. "You're not supposed to be here."

"I... followed you," he croaked. "I had... to make sure

you… were all right. I had to… keep my promise. I didn't… do it… for forgiveness, just… to see that you… are safe."

You were the feeling… You were the tingle down the back of my neck, certain we were not alone. That was why it had not been a sensation of terror. Somehow, Caroline had known that whatever was watching, whatever was following her and her sister, it did not have bad intentions. *He* did not have bad intentions.

She shook her head, stricken at the sight of blood seeping through her handkerchief. "No… no, no, no. You shouldn't have come here. You should have stayed in Leeds, where *you* would be safe." She glanced back over her shoulder, to where Esther stood at the top of the stairs, ashen faced. "Estie, fetch a physician. There must be plenty of them around here. That one that came to see Lambkin when she was a baby—he lived nearby. Don't cease until you find someone! Please, hurry!"

Esther seemed to snap out of her horrified trance, taking off down the stairs with purpose in her step. She sprinted out through the still-open door and turned left, her shouts of "Help! I need help! A doctor! Where is a doctor?" echoing back as she disappeared from view.

"No!" Luke hissed, his face contorting in pain. "Not a physician—she needs to… bring the constables!"

"I don't think that would be wise," Caroline replied, staring across to where Quentin lay, his neck bent at an awkward angle. "I think he's dead, Luke. If the constables come, they won't believe it was an accident."

"Dead?" Luke frowned.

Caroline nodded.

"I suppose that… won't look too… innocent, will it?" Luke mumbled. "But… it was worth it. You can… get your ma out of here. You can start afresh. You can… do all the things you deserve to. She's his...wife. She just became... very wealthy."

Caroline shook her head, holding him closer, gently stroking his soft hair. "I never cared about wealth. I *don't* care about it. I just want me and Esther and Mama and you to go back to Leeds, to Fox House, to look after those children."

"Me too?" He gazed up at her, blinking slowly. "How hard... did I hit my head?"

She tutted under her breath. "Don't jest," she said, her throat choked. "It's not funny. I want you to return with us. I... won't let you die here, so... so... don't you dare. I'm not finished with you. I haven't forgiven you, and you can't die until I have, so... just you stay with me."

"I don't... deserve to be forgiven," he said in a strained voice. "But I am going... to tell you that... I love you. Since the moment... I saw you making... your wish at that well, I think I... started to love you. I'd throw myself... out of a carriage and fall down those stairs... again if I had to, because... there's nothing I wouldn't do... for the woman that I love."

Caroline blinked, a drop of moisture falling onto her cheek. She did not wipe the tear away; she just gazed at him as she pleaded with the heavens to spare him. *I will forgive him, I promise, if you let him survive this. Please, Lord, let him live and I will forgive him.*

"I'm not expecting... a reply, love," he whispered, mistaking her silence.

She loved him too. She had loved him for a while. It was why his betrayal had stung so much, and why she could not bear the thought of being without him, torn in half by the conflict of loving him and resenting him all at once. But faced with the potential loss of him, any lingering anger or resentment had faded like morning fog burned away by summer sunlight.

"I did the same thing," she murmured, picturing Esther's hurt expression. "I kept the same secret because I couldn't find the words or the right time. I had days to tell Esther, and I didn't. I knew it would destroy her."

Luke's breathing became laboured, his eyes shining with pain.

"And... I believe that you tried," she continued, thinking back. "I remember the way you paused during the wedding. I knew there was something you wanted to say. You were... in an impossible position. Quentin *would* have blamed it on you, and you would be in a prison now if you had spoken up. I... think I see that now."

His hand curled around hers. "You don't... have to forgive me. You don't have to make... excuses."

"But you were just another victim," she said with a startling realisation. "You were intimidated into silence. I don't have to make excuses; the reasons are already there."

He turned his head and pressed a trembling kiss to her hand.

A moment later, he went limp, his head lolling to the side, his eyes rolling back as his eyelids fluttered shut.

"No! Luke, no!" she cried out, shaking him. "Wake up! Please, wake up! I didn't get to tell you. I didn't get to tell you that I love you too! Luke, please..."

But he did not move, his head a lifeless weight on her lap, his mouth slack and bloodless.

"Luke!" she howled, not knowing if he was dead or just unconscious, though the sight of him suggested the worst.

To add insult to wretched injury, footsteps thudded on the porch steps and, what felt like a moment too late, Esther came running in with a physician in tow. And behind her, three constables who took one look at the situation and surged forwards, hauling Caroline out of the way, away from the man she loved. A man who might never know just how much.

* * *

"Do you think we haven't seen this countless times before?" one of the constables said with a sneer, standing over Caroline and Esther who kneeled on the floor, their hands bound. "A robbery gone awry."

Caroline shook her head, tears streaming down her face. "We weren't stealing. That man tried to attack us, and my… friend was saving us from harm. They fell. It was an accident. It was all a… horrible accident."

"We hate our stepfather," Esther interjected, scowling at the constables, "but we wouldn't kill him. Do *you* think I'd be stupid enough to call for help if we wanted him dead?"

The constable frowned at that. "I don't know how stupid you are."

"Yes, well, not *that* foolish," Esther muttered, her gaze drifting to Luke.

The physician seemed to be tending to him, despite the situation, moving between Luke and Quentin with a worried frown upon his face.

"We aren't killers, but that man there—Quentin Rawle—*he* killed a man," Caroline said, aware that this might be her sole opportunity to reveal the truth. "He killed our father so that he could marry our mother. Do you know of the portraitist, Adam Calder? *He* is our father. Quentin ran him down with a carriage, on purpose, out of pure jealousy. A few years ago."

The constable's eyes widened, staring at Caroline with a sudden intensity. "I *knew* you looked familiar."

Wondering if he was one of the constables she had spoken to on the day of the accident, Caroline wracked her brain to try and place him.

"Those paintings," the constable turned to his associates. "A month or so ago. Do you remember them?"

One of the other men gasped. "That's her! That's... both of them!"

"What are you talking about?" Caroline asked, frowning.

"There was a theft. All the property of Adam Calder. We caught the miscreants at a warehouse on the docks," the constable explained, his entire demeanour shifting to one of delight. "The paintings were being held by your father's curator, due to be displayed at the London Gallery in the winter of this year. Paintings no one had seen. They were all stolen. Took twenty of us constables to retrieve them."

"What?" Caroline stared at the man in disbelief.

"There were paintings of the two of you. I *knew* I recognised you." The constable beamed as if he had not just bound her hands together and accused her of robbing Quentin's townhouse. "And there were a few of a woman. Is that your mother, do you think?"

Caroline cleared her throat. "I would have to see them." At that moment, she remembered her mother, still lying on the landing. "My mother is up there. Please, someone help her. She has been treated terribly by Quentin. *That* is why we came to rescue her."

The constable nodded to one of his men, who promptly ascended the stairs. When he reached the landing, his cry of surprise rippled down to the entrance hall.

"Get that physician up here!" the man shouted. "There's a woman. At least, I think it's a woman."

"Wait!" Caroline yelped. "Doctor, are either of those two men alive?"

The physician got to his feet, sweeping a hand through his hair. "Both are alive, though one is in better condition than the other." He gestured to Luke. "This one."

Thank goodness... Caroline breathed a small sigh of relief, watching anxiously as the physician traipsed wearily up the stairs. His gasp of horror matched the constable's, his hand flying to his mouth as he stared down at the living skeleton that had once been a vibrant, happy woman.

"Do you have a cart outside?" the physician called down to the constables. "I will need to take at least two of these people to St. Bart's."

"We can take them," the constable who had mentioned the paintings replied.

The physician nodded, looking for a moment like he might be sick. "This lady and the older gentleman will need transportation. If you would help me, I would be very grateful."

"We'll move them," the constable replied, speaking to his associate in a quieter voice, "We'll want the man healed so we can talk to him about the crimes this lady is accusing him of. Might be that he has something to do with those stolen paintings, too."

But as the two in the entrance hall approached Quentin to pick him up and take him out to the cart, he suddenly jumped to his feet. His eyes shone with the gleam of a madman, panic etched across his face, as he darted for the door. Evidently, he had not been in as terrible condition as they thought, merely biding his time so he could make his escape.

As he ran for the door, his injuries became more obvious. He hobbled, limping as fast as he could, panting hard with the exertion and pain, holding his arm to his chest.

The first constable seized him with ease, but it took the efforts of the second constable to restrain Quentin. He fought with all his strength, no doubt realising that if he was captured, he would have to answer for the terrible things he had done.

"Unhand me!" Quentin snarled. "It is my cousin that you want! He is the one who wanted the paintings stolen!"

The constables exchanged a pointed look, as one roughly pulled Quentin's arms behind his back, binding his wrists together. "I think we ought to take *you* to the constabulary first, then on to Newgate. You'll have your time to say all you need to say at the Old Bailey."

"I was forced to do it!" Quentin wailed. "It was my cousin! It was all my cousin!"

He continued to shout and protest, all the way to the adapted Hackney carriage that waited on the street outside. There, Caroline could see him being thrown into the back of the carriage, the doors slamming on his objections.

When the first constable—the one who seemed proud that he knew of Adam Calder—returned inside, he went directly to the sisters, untying their wrists, apologetic in his manner.

"If I'd known who you were, I wouldn't have dared to restrain you," the constable said. "If I'd known the condition your mother was in, I'd have believed you faster."

Caroline rubbed her wrists. "What will you do with Quentin?"

"It depends on what we can get him to confess to, but he's already halfway there," the constable replied. "I'll have someone send word to you if news comes that he's to stand trial."

"Make sure you get him to confess to the murder of my father," Caroline urged, grabbing the constable's hands. "That's all we care about."

The constable nodded. "I'll do what I can." He pointed his chin in the direction of Luke. "You ought to do the same for him. Looks like you owe him for saving your life."

"You won't take him to St. Bart's?" Caroline turned imploring eyes towards the physician, who was descending the stairs with Heather in his arms. She looked so small and thin, more of an otherworldly creature than a person, bundled in those ragged blankets.

The doctor shook his head. "He doesn't require it. He'll awaken in time, if my assessment is correct. The fall knocked him out, that is all."

Caroline wanted to point out that the physician's assessment of Quentin had been the very opposite of correct, but she held her tongue. In truth, she did not want to let Luke leave her sight, fearful that she might never see him again. It was almost the same for her mother, but it was obvious to everyone that Heather desperately needed to be taken to a hospital, where more physicians could tend to her.

"Just watch over him," the physician continued. "Ensure that he rests but be cautious of him becoming disoriented or if he behaves as if he is inebriated. If that should happen, to do not hesitate to call upon me again." He paused, looking a little shy. "I... have one of your father's paintings myself. It is my wife's favourite. So, if I can help further, it would be my honour."

Lumbering to her feet, Caroline moved to take hold of her mother's limp, bony hand. "We'll be waiting for you,

Mama. You need to go with these men and get better, but we'll be right here, and we'll visit just as soon as we can."

"I am getting... my medicine?" her mother replied with a dazed smile.

Caroline swallowed thickly. "You are getting help, Mama." She stared at the physician. "Do not allow anyone to give her laudanum again, no matter how fervently she asks for it. Am I understood?"

"She has an aversion to it?" The physician seemed confused.

Esther jumped in, nodding. "Yes, a terrible aversion. It makes her very, *very* sick. So, don't let her have a single drop."

"Of course." The physician dipped his head in a polite bow and slowly exited the townhouse with Heather, the constables filing out after them.

But not before that first constable turned and, with a friendly wave, said, "Your father's exhibition begins next week. It ought to be very popular, especially considering the scandal of the theft and... the obvious. You should go—the paintings of the two of you are the best ones." He hesitated. "I only glimpsed them, but I remember thinking, those two girls must be dearly beloved."

With that, he left, closing the door politely behind him. Evidently, none of the constables had realised—or had forgotten—that the townhouse was not Caroline and Esther's home.

"I think that means we have somewhere to stay," Esther said, nudging Caroline in the ribs.

Caroline nodded. "I think it does." She glanced down at Luke, relieved to see his eyes flicking back and forth beneath his eyelids. "Come on, help me get him into the

THE CHILD SHE NEVER SPOKE OF

drawing room. It won't be elegant, but I think we can manage it between us."

"We can't just leave him there until he wakes up?" Esther pulled a face. "Put a few blankets over him?"

Despite everything, Caroline laughed. "No, we can't."

"You're going to sit next to him all day and night until he opens his pretty grey eyes, aren't you?" Esther asked with a lopsided grin.

"It's the least I can do."

Esther put an arm around Caroline's waist, leaning into her. "Does this mean you've forgiven him?"

Caroline did not reply.

"If you haven't, you should," Esther insisted. "Marry him, love him, have twenty babies for me to adore and be the best auntie to, and be happy."

Caroline rolled her eyes. "That is quite enough of that." She pulled away from her sister and moved closer to Luke. "Let us keep him alive first, eh?"

"Very well," Esther replied with an eye-roll of her own, as she swept forward to help. "By the way, I think we *should* go and see Papa's exhibition."

A shiver ran down Caroline's spine at the mere thought. Even after almost four years, she did not know if she was ready to face the memories of the past, and the lost possibilities of what could have been. Her father had always hoped to have an exhibition one day; it would not be the same to see it without him.

"Perhaps," she murmured, scooping her hands underneath Luke's arms.

Right now, she was more concerned with the living… and ensuring they stayed that way.

CHAPTER 25

"Did you ever think you would come back to this place?" Esther asked, shadows dancing across her face, cast by the candlelight that flickered on the dining table.

Caroline chewed a mouthful of succulent beef, shaking her head. "I never thought I'd see this house or Mama again. I certainly never thought I'd be eating dinner at this table."

"It's taking all the willpower I possess not to scratch rude words into it." Esther grinned, popping a crisp, buttery potato into her mouth.

It was fortuitous that Caroline's years at Fox House had taught her how to be a reasonably talented cook, with Rosemary as her strict educator. Upon finding a cut of beef, fresh vegetables, and a full pantry at the townhouse, she had decided that the best thing they could do whilst they were waiting for Luke to wake up was to eat.

"Goodness, I can't remember the last time I had beef," Caroline said with a contented sigh. "Or vegetables that didn't taste *slightly* of mould."

"Me neither." Esther nibbled on a roasted carrot, drinking it down with a glass of fresh, cloudy lemonade. A true luxury, discovered in the pantry. "It makes you wonder why Quentin didn't bother to feed Mama. Or why the housekeeper didn't."

The housekeeper had not returned, much to Caroline's relief, and there did not seem to be any other members of staff in the household. She suspected that Quentin had wanted to keep the condition of his wife a secret, burdening the housekeeper with the duties of a maid, a cook, and a confidante.

"If I were to guess," Caroline said carefully, "I would say that Quentin grew tired of Mama. I imagine she did not match the fantasy that he had conjured about her for so many years. So, he left her to rot."

"Are you angry with her?" Esther asked suddenly.

Caroline pressed her lips together in contemplation. "No, I don't think so." She paused. "I keep trying to imagine how I would feel if the man I loved was taken away so cruelly. I would be quite insane. I would seek anything that could temper the pain of it. I blame the 'medicine' but I don't blame her."

"Even though she didn't know us today?" Esther's voice cracked, her chin dropping to her chest.

Caroline nodded. "Even so." She glanced at her sister. "Are *you* angry with her?"

"A little." Esther shrugged. "Maybe it's because I don't know love like that, but... if I were ever a mother, I can't think of any instance that would compel me to forget about my children. I would fight tooth and nail for them. I *definitely* would not marry the next wastrel that came along."

Caroline *had* thought it odd that her younger sister had not tried to say anything to Heather as the physician had carried her out. Now, she understood a little better: it was not merely Heather who had some healing to do. The past three-and-a-half years could not be swept under the rug, and it appeared that Esther was not ready to consider forgiveness.

"Lambkin is gone, Caro," Esther added sadly. "I still think it's for the best, but... Mama didn't try to get us back. I doubt she even remembers she has a third daughter."

"We don't know that she didn't try," Caroline replied evenly. "We weren't here. We didn't see what Mama was like in the aftermath. Maybe, she attempted to escape and come after us. We'll have to ask her when she is feeling better."

Esther sniffed. "You can do that. I don't intend to visit her."

"As you prefer." Caroline smiled sadly, hating that it had come to this. It was a snarled knot of pain and resentment and regret and so many things unspoken and unknown, and she did not have the first idea of how to untangle it.

With time, she told herself. *Time will fix this.*

If she were back at the garden next to Sadler's Wells Theatre, that was what she would have wished for—for time and patience to fix what had been broken.

* * *

"Estie!" Caroline shouted frantically, bursting through the door of the room that her sister had commandeered. "Estie, wake up!"

Esther cracked open one disapproving eye. "What's wrong?"

"Luke is gone," Caroline gasped, heart racing. "I woke up in the drawing room, and he wasn't there."

Esther sat bolt upright. "What do you mean?"

"I mean, he's not there!" Caroline urged. "I think… I think he left."

And I think it's my fault for not telling him that I forgive him, and that I love him too. She could not help blaming herself for falling asleep whilst she was supposed to be keeping watch over him, either. She had tried to stay awake, she really had, but her eyelids had gotten heavier and heavier, and she supposed she must have dozed off at some point.

"Have you searched the house?" Esther rubbed her eyes.

"I've searched everywhere." Caroline pressed the heel of her hand into her chest, but it did nothing to loosen the tight feeling that gripped her lungs. "I can't find him, Estie. And if he left without a word, I don't even know if I *should* try to find him."

Esther threw back the coverlets. "He hit his head, Caro. We *absolutely* need to find him. The physician said to make sure he didn't become disoriented. It might be that he didn't know where he was, got confused, and wandered out of the house."

She had an excellent point.

"Dress swiftly," Caroline said. "Meanwhile, I shall try to think of anywhere he might have gone to."

Esther stifled a yawn. "I shan't be long."

Caroline hurried back out, pausing to lean against the nearest wall and catch her breath. It had been an awful shock to wake up and find Luke absent, his blankets pushed aside, the indent of his head still in the cushion where he had rested. She had not meant to fall asleep. She should not have done. She should have pinched herself to stay awake, done more to ensure that she kept her vigil over him.

Gathering herself, Caroline headed along the hallway and trudged slowly down the stairs, still as weary as if she had not slept at all.

Just then, she heard a sound, coming from the rear of the house. The kitchens, if she was not mistaken. The scuff of footfalls and the creak of hinges.

Heart thudding, she ran the rest of the way down the stairs, half-slipping on the tiles of the entrance hall, not stopping until she burst through the kitchen doors.

Luke sat beside the door that led into the immaculate gardens. A weighty saucepan held the door open, whilst he enjoyed the light breeze that swept in from the overcast morning outside.

He turned to look at her, a frown forming on his brow. "What's the matter?"

"I... thought you were gone. I thought you'd left us," she gasped. "Left... me."

His frown relaxed. "I saw you sleeping and didn't want to disturb you, so I thought I would explore the gardens. They're beautiful. I haven't seen that much greenery in years." He mustered a smile. "I dozed off in the pagoda. Didn't mean to worry anyone, least of all you."

Caroline ran to him, throwing her arms around him before she could stop herself. She held him tightly, all the fear and concern draining out of her as she felt his arms slide around her in return, the faint press of his smile against her shoulder.

"You're an idiot," she mumbled. "You shouldn't be walking around in your condition."

"My condition?" He laughed. "What condition is that?"

"You were knocked unconscious," she said, pulling

back. "You have a gash across your head, the physician said I was to watch you closely and that you were to rest when you woke up. Don't you remember what happened?"

He smiled up at her, pulling her into his lap. "I remember perfectly well, and I *feel* perfectly well. A slight headache, sure, but otherwise fine." The gleam in his eyes dimmed for a moment. "What about Quentin? Did he…"

"He was arrested," Caroline replied. "Remarkably alive, and guilty of more than we knew. If he confesses, he will be charged with the crime of grand larceny. I don't know that he will confess to killing my father, but at least he will never see daylight again."

Luke lifted his hand to Caroline's cheek, brushing his thumb across the apple. "He *will* confess, Caro." He expelled a deep sigh. "I'll go to the constabulary today, and the magistrate after if I must, to tell them what I know and what I saw. I will do what I should have done years ago."

"But… you are hurt," she murmured, holding his face in return.

He shook his head. "I don't think you were listening before, Caro. There is nothing I wouldn't do for the woman I love."

"I was listening," she said softly. "But you fell unconscious before you heard my response."

He raised an eyebrow. "Oh?"

"I love you too." Her heart swelled, leaping with nervous excitement. "I love you, and I… forgive you. It hurt me, I won't deny that, but I understand what it is like to be trapped by the threats of powerful men. You were just another victim, same as me and Esther and Mama and Lambkin."

Luke's eyes widened as if he had just remembered something. "How *is* your mother? What happened to her?"

"The physician took her to St. Bart's. I mean to visit her today." She gave a small, shy shrug. "Perhaps, we could walk together. It is not far from the Old Bailey."

He smiled. "Of course, love. But there's something I must do first…"

"What is that?"

He cradled her cheek, rising up slightly in the chair. As he came up, she bent her head, closing her eyes as their lips met in a soft graze. She melted into the moment, her heart brimming with contentment as she kissed him deeply, the cool morning breeze swirling around them, bringing in the scent of roses and jasmine.

He kissed her back in kind, holding her close, his lips guiding her through any nerves or hesitation, until it felt like the most natural thing in the world. Something that had always been fated, though it had taken them a while to realise it. And though she had never wished for him, or wished for a man like him, she was grateful that the heavens themselves had understood what she needed and sent him to her.

"I see you found him," Esther's voice said from the kitchen doorway, laced with amusement.

Caroline drew back abruptly, though Luke kept his arm around her, laughing at the interruption.

"I… We… It…" Caroline tried to say, her words abandoning her.

Esther grinned. "No, no—no need to explain. All I can say is, about bloody time."

CHAPTER 26

It was not difficult for Caroline to find her mother at St. Bartholomew's Hospital; she could hear the shrieks and shouts from the main entrance, following them all the way up to a solitary room where, evidently, Heather had been placed in order to avoid disturbing the other people who were suffering. A tactic that had not worked.

It had been two days since Luke had woken up, the new residents of Quentin's townhouse deciding that it would be for the best if they rested and recuperated instead of traipsing across London.

"You should wait a while before you see your mother," Luke had insisted. *"She'll need time to recuperate too. It takes time for the effects of the laudanum to fade, especially considering she has been drinking it for such a long while."*

He had intended to visit the constabulary anyway, but the constable who had saved the paintings had come by to inform Caroline and Esther that Quentin had been charged with grand larceny and would face trial in the coming week. Luke had asked to speak with the man, and they had gone into the drawing room together for some time, and when they had emerged, there had been a silent accord between the two men.

"What did you say to him?" Caroline had asked.

"Quentin will face punishment for another crime," Luke had replied, kissing her. *"The magistrate will be informed. You will have your justice, if it's the last thing I do."*

"Don't let it be," Caroline had said with a smile, kissing him back.

As Caroline opened the door to her mother's room, an overwhelming sense of anxiety struck her. Esther had stayed at the townhouse, telling her sister that she was not yet ready to see their mother, and Caroline wondered if, perhaps, she should have left it a while longer. Clearly, her mother was in no condition for visitors.

"You!" Heather pointed a bony finger at Caroline, apparently unable to recognise her own daughter. "My medicine! Give me my medicine! I need it. I am sick—I need it!"

Caroline edged further into the room. "You can't have it." She willed confidence into her voice. "The medicine is what has made you sick."

"I need it!" Heather wailed. "It hurts too much without it!"

Caroline stepped ever closer. "I'm not giving it to you. It... ruined our lives, Mama. It ruined all of our lives."

Heather frowned, staring at Caroline with an intensity that unnerved her. "I know you..."

"Yes, you do." Caroline took a breath. "It's me, Mama. Caroline."

Heather shook her head vigorously. "No, you're lying. It's not you. It can't be you. You left me—you took Esther and you left me. You ran away."

"Is that what Quentin told you?"

"Quentin?" Heather's face contorted into a mask of disgust. "Don't speak to me of him. I despise him. He wouldn't let me pursue my girls. He wouldn't let me find my girls. He locked me up, he starved me, he punished me, until I forgot my girls. But you're not my daughter. You went away and you didn't come back."

Caroline sat down on the edge of the bed, not yet brave enough to take her mother's hand. Her heart ached as she stared at her mother, realising that she had been somewhat right in her suspicions—her mother *had* tried to retrieve her daughters, and had suffered for it. Yet, it hurt her heart all the more to note that there was no mention of Lambkin.

"Quentin *took* us away," Caroline said, explaining the story as quickly as she could, before her mother got distracted by thoughts of her medicine again. She explained about the morning after her birthday, the journey north, their arrival at Fox House, the textile mill, and how hard she had been forced to strive to keep Lambkin with them.

Her mother turned up her nose. "Who is Lambkin? I don't know a Lambkin. What sort of name is that?"

"She is your daughter, Mama! She is your daughter, and that is her name because you didn't bother to name her!" Caroline replied, losing patience. "She is three years old, and she… was given to someone else because Quentin wrote a letter declaring that you wanted nothing to do with her! I am aware that he orchestrated this, but *you* should have the decency to at least remember her! Instead, you are crying out for the medicine that allowed you to forget her in the first place."

Heather fell silent, an expression of shock upon her face as she recoiled into the wrought-iron headboard of her bed. She stared at Caroline with recognition and fear, clasping her hands together as if she meant to pray. For forgiveness, perhaps. For her forgotten daughter, maybe.

"I had a little girl," she whispered, but whether it was a question or a statement, Caroline did not know.

"You did."

Heather frowned. "She... wouldn't stop crying."

"Because of the medicine," Caroline told her. "Your need for it became her need for it, and she screamed because she could not have it—because she was feeling the way you are now, in the first days and weeks and months of her life."

Horror rippled across Heather's face. "The... medicine hurt her?"

"I am no physician, but I have been told that it's not uncommon," Caroline replied, forcing herself to be calmer.

"W-Where is she?" Heather croaked.

"I told you; she is with a pleasant couple who have adopted her." Caroline flinched inwardly, wondering if she would ever be fully at ease with the reality. "Esther and I came back for you to help you, but you must also help yourself. Whether or not Lambkin can be retrieved relies upon that. I'm not even sure it's possible now, but... it certainly won't be if you don't get better."

In that moment, Caroline's mother crumbled. Her thin body began to shake, tears beading on her lashes, tumbling down onto her sunken cheeks. Her lip trembled, her bony chest rising and falling frantically as she sucked in jarring breaths.

"What have I done?" Heather mumbled, rubbing her eyes. "How could I have... let this happen?"

Caroline sighed. "You were grief-stricken. You were struggling. Quentin scared you into thinking you would be impoverished and desperate without his assistance and then gave you so much of that 'medicine' that you could not have made a decision for yourself, even if you had wanted to." She shook her head. "But it isn't too late to fix it. Papa has an exhibition now, at the London Gallery. There will be money for you somewhere, I imagine, if we speak to the right people. *And* you are entitled to everything that was Quentin's. When he is imprisoned, it will be yours."

Of course, there had been no trial yet, so nothing was assured, but Caroline clung to the hope that Quentin would be sentenced and thrown in a prison for a very, *very* long time. She did not want to exist in a world where that was not the outcome.

"Imprisoned?" Heather squinted.

"For his greed," Caroline replied, telling her mother the abridged version of recent and past events.

Heather stared unblinking at her eldest daughter, when the story was finished. "He... killed my love? He stole... my love's paintings?"

"He did, just as he sold us unlawfully to his cousin," Caroline said, her patience fraying once more.

Heather burst into fresh tears, hiding her face in her skeletal hands. Her shoulders shuddered as she wept, and as her wails of anguish filled the gloomy room, Caroline finally reached out and took hold of her mother's hand. She pulled it away from her mother's face and gave the thin fingers a reassuring squeeze, hoping to let her know that all was not lost.

This grief is not as new to me. Have patience, be gracious.

No matter how many years had passed, or what Heather had once been aware of, it was as if she had just been told that her husband had died. The agony and devastation was a visceral onslaught that tugged at Caroline's heart, conjuring tears in her eyes that rolled freely down her cheeks.

"I'm sorry," Heather choked at last, gripping Caroline's hand with surprising strength. "I'm so sorry that I... abandoned you all. I'm sorry I didn't see... until it was too late, that Quentin was a monster. I'm sorry I didn't try harder to get you back. I'm... I'm so very sorry. Oh, Caro, I'm so sorry. Where is Esther? I must apologise to her too."

Caroline smiled sadly. "She didn't want to come. She's not ready yet. There's... a lot of anger that she needs to contend with. Be patient with her."

"Yes... yes, of course," Heather murmured, wiping her face. "H-How could she possibly... forgive me? I don't know that I'll be able to forgive myself."

Caroline wanted to tell her that this was not about her, but she did not have the heart. Heather had just learned that her dearest love had been killed by her current husband, and she had lost one of her daughters to strangers: it was no time for a chiding.

"I will get better," Heather said, her voice a note stronger. "I will get better, and I will... get my baby girl back. I promise."

Caroline nodded slowly. "I hope so."

"I mean it." Heather's breath caught in her throat. "Now, my dear girl, if you don't mind... I should like to be alone for a while."

A frown creased Caroline's brow. "For how long?"

"A while," her mother replied. "A few days. In truth, maybe it would be for the best if... you didn't come back here. I will come to you, when I am allowed to leave. I will show you that I intend to be better, and that I mean to... undo as much of what I have done as I can."

Caroline gave her mother's hand one more squeeze.

"We'll be waiting, Mama. We have been waiting, all this time, for you to say that."

Though she did not want to leave her mother on her own, despite her conflicted feelings surrounding the troubled woman, Caroline suspected it might be the best course of action. Her mother was certainly clearer in her mind, and understood the enormity of what her medicine-induced oblivion had caused—she needed to prove to herself, more than anything, that she *could* overcome her desire for laudanum and keep her promise.

"We'll be waiting," Caroline repeated. "I am trusting you, Mama, not to let us down."

She got up and headed back out into the hallway, closing the door behind her, leaving her mother alone to wage war against her demons and her grief, hopefully once and for all.

CHAPTER 27

"Quentin Peter Rawle, I hereby sentence you to transportation for the crime of grand larceny and the manslaughter of Adam Calder," the judge declared, banging down his gavel.

Some boos echoed down from the gallery, the public thirsty for an execution, but it seemed that Quentin had managed to weasel his way out of the crime of murder with some clever lies—telling just enough of the truth to lessen his punishment. Even with Luke's testimony about what had happened on the day Adam died, it had made little difference. After all, Quentin was still considered to be a gentleman and a man of power, whilst Luke was no one of merit. Not to those who cast judgement, at least. Luke could not even prove that he was Quentin's son.

"Take him away," the judge commanded, as the court bailiffs seized Quentin by the arms and dragged him down from the dock. Quentin struggled, of course, and shouted something incoherent about his cousin, but the din of the crowd was too loud to hear it.

As Quentin disappeared out of a door at the rear of the

courthouse, Luke turned to Caroline and Esther, who sat beside him on the front row of the gallery.

"Is it enough?" he asked.

Esther sniffed. "As long as his ship sinks on his way to the other side of the world, then yes."

"It is enough," Caroline said with a relieved smile. True, it was *not* what she had hoped for exactly, but knowing that Quentin would never set foot on English soil again and would suffer the degradation and struggles of transportation *did* feel like justice served.

Luke took hold of Caroline's hand. "Come on. We ought to celebrate."

They shuffled out of the gallery, filing out of the courthouse with the rest of the rabble. The trial had been perversely popular, though perhaps it should not have been so unexpected, considering Adam Calder's increased fame. Having been in Leeds for so long, Caroline had not been there to witness her father's posthumous rise to much-beloved artist. Of course, he had been famous when he was alive, but only within a certain circle of people. Now, his success had widened beyond belief; it was just a terrible shame that he was not there to enjoy it.

Outside, London had transformed beneath the golden glow of afternoon sunlight, the air balmy, the entire city's mood somehow lifted by the pleasant weather. Or, perhaps, it was because Caroline's own mood had lifted that she saw more of the joy that could be found, if one only cared to look closely enough.

"I asked after your mother," Luke said as they made their way down to the river, wandering westward along the Thames. The sluggish water glittered in the beautiful sunlight, though there was little of merit to be said about the scent.

Esther turned her gaze away, pretending not to care. Caroline knew that her sister did, deep down, but she had always had a stubborn streak. And there was still a lot to forgive, and no notion of whether or not Heather would keep her promises.

It had been over a week since Caroline had visited her mother at St. Bart's, and every time she heard someone walk by the townhouse or a carriage rattle by, she willed it to be Heather, coming back to them.

"Is she well?" Caroline asked.

Luke nodded. "According to the physician I spoke to. She's improving day by day."

"Any word as to when she might be able to leave?" Caroline struggled to keep the anticipation out of her voice.

Luke shook his head. "No specifics. But... I thought you'd want to know."

"Thank you, love," Caroline said, resting her head on Luke's shoulder as they continued to wander in an unknown direction, a weight seemingly lifted from all of them. "Was it enough for you—that punishment?"

Quentin was your father, after all... she neglected to add. It did not need to be said.

Luke nodded. "If it was enough for the two of you, it was plenty for me."

Falling into a companionable, peaceful silence, they continued on along the riverbank in the summer glow. Only when they turned northward again, Luke gently leading the way, did Caroline begin to grow suspicious of where they might be going.

She glimpsed the sky-grazing top of Nelson's Column, splitting the view of Trafalgar Square in half, and knew precisely where they were headed. She had been in the Wilkins Building a few times in her childhood to see the paintings that were being exhibited, so it was not new to her, but fear slowed her pace as they got closer and closer.

"Your father's works are in there," Luke said quietly. "You should see them."

Caroline swallowed thickly. "I don't know if I can."

"That's why we didn't tell you," Esther interjected with a smile, looping her arm through Caroline's. "I realise I'm being a hypocrite, since I refuse to face Mama, but... I think this will be good for you. They're beautiful, Caro. You *must* see them."

Caroline glanced down at her sister. "You have seen them already?"

Esther nodded.

"When?"

"When you went to see Mama," Esther replied, a little shamefaced. "They were still preparing the exhibition, but they allowed me in. So, in a way, I am seeing it for the first time too."

Carried along by the man she loved and her sister, Caroline steeled her courage and allowed them to lead her across the square and up the steps, into the gallery.

They were not alone as they entered, a veritable crowd filtering through the exhibition halls with them. The trio ignored the usual fare, passing straight through to the hall that Caroline feared and looked forward to in equal measure.

"Close your eyes," Luke said, as they came to the doors of that particular hall.

Caroline nodded, obeying as her heart thundered in her chest.

"I won't let you trip," he murmured, laughter in his voice, as he guided her forward.

She took perhaps twelve steps, listening to the chatter

all around her, the gasps and plaudits of other visitors, the compliments and commentaries that would have made her father so happy. A knot in her chest began to unravel—a knot that had been so tightly twisted that she had never thought it would loosen, no matter what she did. The complicated tangle of her grief, that she had pushed down for so long, for the sake of her sisters and her mother.

And as she stood there, eyes scrunched shut, a sob made its way up her throat, emerging as a stifled choke. Tears snuck from the corners of her eyes, and she tasted the salt of them in her mouth.

"Open them," Luke encouraged.

Pulling her beloved and her sister closer, Caroline did just that, her eyes flying wide to take in the exhibition all around her. It was the best kind of bombardment, not knowing what to look at first: the extraordinary countryside and city landscapes that her father had painted when he was bored; the portraits of noble families and friends; the horses and dogs that he had painted so regally; or the collection of paintings that took up all of the southern wall, of two young girls, growing steadily into young women.

"When did he paint these?" Caroline murmured to herself, approaching those portraits: pictures of her and Esther, unaware that they were being put to memory or immortalised on canvas.

There were seven in all. The first was of Esther as a baby, arms stretching up from her cradle, with Caroline peering over.

I must have been four or so...

The second was an infant Esther walking clumsily towards her older sister; the third of them sitting together on a bench in Hyde Park; the fourth of Esther sitting on Caroline's shoulders as they wandered away from the painter; the fifth of them both looking less than impressed, walking out of Frances Buss's school; and the sixth was of them—the three of them, daughters and mother—at the kitchen table laughing over something that Caroline could not remember.

But the seventh picture was familiar sketch of the two sisters drawing. A sketch that Caroline had left under her pillow, and thought lost.

Just then, she noticed a series of paintings, smaller than the rest, but so intricate and detailed that Caroline expected them to come to life at any moment. It was three portraits, depicting the same woman: portraits of Heather standing at a window, beautifully illuminated, her belly slightly rounded. She wore different clothing in each, but her expression was the same, as was her pose—head turned back to look at the painter, a smile on her face, her hand resting on her swollen belly as if to say, *"Look, my love. Look what we have created."*

"Oh..." Caroline covered her mouth with her hand, her eyes stinging. "Oh... Papa."

Esther put her arms around Caroline. "He loved us so much." Her voice cracked. "He loved *her* so much."

"He did," Caroline croaked, hugging Esther to her.

The sisters stood like that for a while, admiring their father's masterpieces, ignoring the whispers and stares that were cast in their direction. Although the girls in the portraits were younger, there was no mistaking them. People noticed, but no one approached, perhaps realising it might not be appropriate.

"If I may," Luke said awkwardly, clearing his throat.

Caroline smiled up at him. "What, my love?"

"There's another reason I brought you here," Luke explained, his throat bobbing. "I realise I can't ask your

THE CHILD SHE NEVER SPOKE OF

father for your hand directly, but... surrounded by his work, I wanted to ask if you would do me the honour of... becoming my wife?"

She pressed her hand to her heart as Esther shrieked with delight. Caroline's heart was already so full, yet Luke's proposal had just made it run over. A wider smile stretched across her face, fresh tears brimming in her eyes, her stomach turning giddy somersaults.

"Yes," she gasped, those happy tears falling as she grabbed Luke's hands and held them tightly. "Yes, my love. Yes, I will marry you!"

Despite the audience and the scandal it might cause, when Luke pulled her to him, she went, throwing her arms around his neck. He held her as if they were about to dance, his eyes shining with happiness, before dipping his head and stealing a sweet kiss from her lips. She kissed him back, knowing with all of her heart that her father would approve. He had always said that they should never settle for less than the most extraordinary love, and here he was —*her* great love, ready and eager to begin their life together.

"I love you," she whispered, pulling back, holding his face.

He smiled. "As I love you, my dearest Caro."

"Yes, well, I adore you both," Esther chimed in, clapping merrily.

The happy couple laughed and pulled her in for a hug: a scene that Caroline wished she had the talent to paint, so it might be captured and immortalised. But her mind and her memory would have to suffice, allowing her to look back with a fond smile, remembering everything exactly as it was.

And, one day, I'll have a portraitist paint us—all of us. For there were two people still missing, the picture incomplete without them.

"What would you say to us marrying in Leeds?" Caroline asked, looking into Luke's beautiful grey eyes.

He smiled as if he had known the question was coming. "I would say, when do we leave?"

CHAPTER 28

One Month Later...

Caroline, Luke, Esther, and Heather arrived at Fox House in time to hear the news that Mr. Fox had been hanged for his crimes of infanticide. The 'Mothers' in his employ had spoken against him in order to save themselves, providing a scathing, appalling account of what Mr. Fox had been doing behind the guise of an 'orphanage.'

Rosemary had also given testimony, as she informed the quartet proudly whilst ushering them into the dining room, "It was fitting, if you ask me," she said, showing them where to sit. "That his miserable life ended the way of his victims—execution. I didn't see his last moments myself, of course. Don't have the stomach for it, and I confess, I'm far too busy here to be bothering over what happens out there." She gestured to the windows, where the sun was just setting across the city, the seasons on the brink of turning, though the heat of summer clung on.

"It feels cheerful in here, Rosemary," Caroline said, listening to the sounds of Fox House.

Children were laughing upstairs and there were boys

playing out in the yard which had been cleared in Caroline's absence. More of the children were out on the 'Green,' causing mischief with the children of those who lived in the buildings surrounding the square.

"I should hope so," Rosemary replied, leaning on the back of a chair. "I've done my best, and I mean to keep it this way. Make it into a proper orphanage. A refuge. I already have the local church's blessing, but I might need some helping hands if you're thinking of coming back for good."

Caroline and Luke exchanged a look, smiling at one another.

"We're not going back to London, that's for certain," Luke said. "In truth, we're getting married, and we're planning to marry right here in Leeds."

Rosemary gasped. "Who is?"

"Caroline and me."

The older woman shrieked so loudly that a couple of the boys playing in the yard ran in to ensure there was nothing wrong. But when they saw Caroline, Esther, and Luke sitting at the table, chaos was unleashed. The boys darted back out, shouting at the top of their lungs, "Miss Caro and Mr. Luke are back! Miss Esther is back! Everyone, come see!"

"I think we ought to brace ourselves," Caroline teased, though Rosemary was the first to smother the happy couple with affection, embracing them excitedly, jostling them, accusing them merrily of trying to make her die of happiness.

A moment later, the children poured in. The dining room filled with noise, the boys and girls fighting to be the first to hug Esther and the prodigal couple, clamouring and complaining and welcoming the trio home.

And as Caroline embraced the two girls who had been Lambkin's dearest friends, she could not deny the change in everyone. No one was nervous to put a foot out of line. No one was waiting for the day they would be carried off, never to be seen again. They looked healthier, they looked happier, they looked like children.

"Right, off with you!" Rosemary commanded, once everyone had had a chance to welcome the trio back. "We've got some talking to do, and it's not yet your dinner time, so go on back to your playing. The weather won't be like this much longer, and you'll be sorry you didn't make the best of it."

Reluctantly, the children filtered back out of the dining room, leaving the 'adults' to their conversation.

"It's an important dinner tonight," Rosemary explained, finally sitting down. "I had this notion about 'adoption dinners,' you see, where prospective parents can come and dine with the littluns, see if they're worthy."

Luke quirked an eyebrow. "The children or the parents?"

Rosemary shot him a mock-withering look. "The parents, of course." Her face relaxed into a smile. "So, you've come back at a good time. Of course, with you getting married, I suppose you won't want to stay here anymore. You'll be wanting your own lodgings, your own work, that sort of thing."

"Who said that?" Caroline grinned. "If you'll have us, we'd be delighted to come back. Indeed, my mother was hoping to make you—well, Fox House—an offer."

Heather had recovered well over the past month, putting on weight, keeping her promise to get better, no longer reliant upon the laudanum. Once she had been permitted to leave the hospital, she had returned to the townhouse. There, of an evening, over dinner, she had listened intently to everyone's stories of Fox House and the children there. So intently and with such admiration that she had, one night, made a suggestion.

"I was hoping I might make a donation to the orphanage," Heather said shyly. "I have... a considerable fortune, and do not want to do anything with it, so... perhaps you would agree to use it for something good. For this place. For those children."

With the aid of an excellent, and rather wily, lawyer, she had managed to receive the inheritance that had been waiting for her since Adam's death—an inheritance she had known nothing about, which had only increased since his posthumous fame. Added to that, in time, would be the money from the sale of Quentin's townhouse, and any belongings within it.

"I can't take charity, Mrs. Calder," Rosemary said, those last two words making Heather's eyes widen.

"Then, might you consider an exchange?" Heather replied, her voice thick. It had undoubtedly been a long time since anyone had called her Mrs. Calder.

Rosemary tilted her head to one side. "What sort of exchange?"

"I give you the donation but, so it isn't *quite* charity, I also help here at Fox House," Heather said. "I could help you to manage it, if you wouldn't be averse to such a thing. It has been years since I have had a purpose, and I should like to have one again."

A grin cracked across Rosemary's face. "Now, *that* I can accept." She expelled a breath of something like relief. "I need all the assistance I can get, though I don't think we ought to call it Fox House anymore. Too many unpleasant memories. I've been thinking for a while about changing the name, so if you've any suggestions, I'd be glad to hear 'em."

"The Calder Orphanage," Esther chimed in, her smile sad. "The donation is coming from my papa's art, so it ought to be named after him."

Rosemary's expression softened. "I like that."

"As do I," Heather murmured, avoiding looking at her middle daughter.

Although some of the ice had thawed between them, there was still some way to go before there was true warmth again. But Caroline saw glimpses of it more and more, with every day that passed. And once they knew if Lambkin could be restored to them, she had no doubt that Heather and Esther would be able to find the comfort in one another that they once had.

"I'm glad to have you here, Mrs. Calder," Rosemary said, somewhat pointedly. "I was praying for you all when you went down to London, praying that they'd be able to save you and bring you here. Of course, you've had me on tenterhooks these past weeks, worrying over what might've happened to you."

"We wanted to wait until Mama was better," Caroline explained. "And we couldn't leave until we saw Quentin's ship depart either, just in case he managed to find a way to sneak off it. But he's on his way to faraway shores now, Mr. Fox is gone, and... I don't want to curse anything by saying so, but I think... everyone is now exactly where they're meant to be."

"Except one," Esther pointed out.

Rosemary sat up straighter in her chair. "You mean the littlun?"

Esther nodded.

"Aye, well, I'm afraid I can't help much with that,"

Rosemary said apologetically. "I don't have any news of her, but now that you're back, you should go and visit her. They said you could, so I don't see why they'd have any argument."

Heather made a strange, strangled noise. "Oh, I should like that. More than anything."

"Then, that's what we'll do," Caroline said with a decisive nod. "Tonight, we'll settle ourselves. Tomorrow, we'll venture to the Hyles' to see how Lambkin is faring, and after that… we'll start enquiries as to how we might be able to get Lambkin back."

After all, so much had changed. At the time, the life that Mr. and Mrs. Hyles had offered had seemed better than any that could be offered to Lambkin by her sisters, but it was not just them now. They had their mother back and, what was more, they had a remarkable fortune at their disposal—aside from that which was earmarked for the orphanage.

"It shouldn't be too difficult," Rosemary said. "There was never any proper contract or anything signed for the adoption. I checked and had the lass across the square who knows her letters better than I do check again for me. Far as I can tell, the Hyles' don't have any right to her, if you tell 'em you want her back."

Caroline stared at Rosemary. "I thought you said you couldn't help much?"

"Aye, I meant with how she was settling into her life with those people," Rosemary replied, wafting a dismissive hand. "I didn't realise you'd be wanting to retrieve her but, if I may, I think it's a fine idea. A child ought to be with family," she gestured around her, "or whatever's closest if there's no family to be had. Now, what do you all say to something to eat and drink? You must be starved and parched after your journey."

Caroline laughed. "There *is* food and refreshment between here and London, you know."

"Maybe, but not the way I make it," Rosemary replied with a wink, as she scraped back her chair and headed into the kitchens, giving them no opportunity to refuse.

* * *

CAROLINE WATCHED from the doorway of the kitchen, her stomach almost as full as her heart. The children were finishing hearty portions of stewed apples and berries, cooled with a small pouring of milk, talking and jesting and humming amongst themselves. Indeed, they seemed mostly oblivious to the slightly nervous couple who sat at the end of the table—potential parents, invited to meet the children and to be judged at a distance by Rosemary.

I wonder if they'll give a happy new life to someone... Caroline could not help but think of Lambkin, her gaze drifting to Esther and Heather, who stood off to one side of the dining room, observing in much the same manner. Mother and daughter were closer than they had dared to be before, side-by-side, comfortable in their mutual task of not-so-discreetly overseeing the 'adoption dinner.'

"I saved you some," Luke's voice warmed Caroline, coming from behind her.

She turned to smile at him, but as she did, he slipped his arm around her waist and pulled her into the kitchens, out of sight of the children and the prospective parents.

"Luke!" she protested playfully, as he held her against his chest.

"I haven't had a moment alone with you all day," he murmured, close to her ear.

She covered his arm with hers. "Nor should you. We're not married yet."

He chuckled. "We *would* be married if you hadn't wanted to wait." He pressed a kiss to her neck and turned her around in his arms. "Are you happy, love?"

"I think so," she replied, gazing into his eyes. "No... I am. It's strange to be here again, but it's wonderful how so much has changed in such a short time. Rosemary has worked miracles."

He nodded. "Did you ever doubt she would, given half a chance?"

"Not at all." She leaned forward, resting against him as he held her. "I can't wait to marry you, my love. I hope you don't think I'm delaying because I'm not happy or excited?"

He laughed softly. "No, love. I understand. You want your family to be together to celebrate our union. Even if Lambkin is probably too young to remember it, it's for *your* memory, not hers."

"Just when I think I couldn't love you more," she said with a contented sigh.

"I adore you both, but if you could show your affection somewhere that isn't my kitchen, I'd be grateful," Rosemary interrupted, coming in from the dining room.

Blushing, Caroline pulled away from Luke. "I was just about to eat my pudding."

"Of course you were." Rosemary laughed to herself. "I think the couple are leaving now, if there's anything you want to say?"

Caroline perked up at that. "Are they interested in adopting any of the children?"

"Olivia and Abigail," Rosemary replied with a somewhat nervous smile.

Abandoning Luke and her bowl of stewed apples, Caroline hurried back out into the dining room. The couple had retreated to the window, putting on their hats and coats, though it was far too warm an evening for the latter. They seemed pleasant, older than the Hyles' had been, wearing clothes that were neither shabby nor too ostentatious.

"I hear you are interested in adopting two of the girls," Caroline blurted out in a hushed tone, careful not to raise the hopes of Olivia and Abigail. Although, she need not have worried; the children were still entirely invested in their apples.

The couple nodded in unison.

"They are such darlings, and they seem to be dear friends," the lady said, her hand to her heart. "I could not dream of separating them."

The gentleman nodded. "They are such bonny girls. Sweet, well-mannered, amusing, and... very talkative." He laughed awkwardly. "Our house has missed that noise terribly."

"You have children of your own?" Caroline asked.

The couple looked at one another.

"We had a son," the gentleman said, his voice thickening. "He died some four years ago, now. It sounds... foolish, perhaps, but my wife and I would like to raise more children, see them grow, but we cannot have more of our own. We are too old, alas."

Caroline realised that their son had likely been a grown man when he passed, and though her heart felt sore for the couple, she could not neglect the care and future of the children at Fox House.

"Take as much time as you need to consider it," she said firmly. "Return in a few days if you are quite serious about your interest, but please do know that, if you choose to adopt them, I *will* check on their welfare from time to time, to ensure that they have the upbringing that they deserve: a happy childhood, loved by people who adore them as if they *were* their own."

The lady smiled, her eyes glittering. "We will take our time, but be assured, if we were to proceed, we would cherish them as if they were born to us."

"We would," the gentleman agreed, his tone bittersweet.

The couple said farewell to the children, who chorused "goodbye" in reply, and Caroline led them back out of Fox House—soon to be the Calder Orphanage. She waved farewell to them from the porch, hoping fervently that they were the good people she thought them to be, and that they would return for Olivia and Abigail soon.

"It's a good idea," Luke said, appearing on the step beside her. "This way, the children get a say too."

Caroline leaned into him as he put his arm around her. "I think this place is finally going to become something... wondrous." She smiled. "The orphans who come here will find care and happiness, and when they leave us, they'll have it wherever they go too."

"No one can ask for more than that." Luke kissed the top of her head. "I know we only just returned, but... it feels like home. Don't you think?"

She peered up at him. "I was just about to say that. Being in London showed me that it's not where I belong anymore. But as soon as I stepped through these doors again... I felt it. I am home. I am with my family, I am with you—I am home."

With her head on his chest, they gazed out at the barren 'Green' together, seeing beauty in every wildflower and weed that sprouted from the dust and debris. Indeed, to Caroline, those stubborn shrubs were a lot like love, appearing when she least expected it, in places she would never have thought to look and, more importantly, it was able to weather any storm that came its way, growing upwards and anchoring its roots downwards, even in adversity.

"I love you," she whispered, slipping her arms around his waist.

He kissed her brow gently. "I love you too."

And as the first star appeared in the twilight sky, Caroline did not make a wish. She did not need to, when she had almost everything that she could have wished for right there, making her happier than she had ever dared to be.

EPILOGUE

"She said it was opposite the grammar school they're constructing, with two stags by the gate," Caroline replied, in answer to the question that her mother had asked for the twentieth time since leaving the orphanage. "I will never forget that, for as long as I live."

Heather fidgeted with the collar of her chemisette, as if it were strangling her. It *was* a feverishly hot day, the summer marking its end in a suitably dramatic display of sweltering discomfort, but Caroline knew there was more to her mother's unrest than the weather.

She is nervous. Dreading it and anticipating it.

"I just want to be certain," Heather said quietly, as the motion of the borrowed cart jostled her from side to side.

Esther rolled her eyes. "Caro wouldn't lead us to the wrong place, Mother."

"No, I know." Heather tugged again at her collar. "Forgive me, I slept poorly."

"It's understandable," Caroline said in a milder tone, for she could not even begin to imagine what was racing through her mother's mind at that moment.

Over the past month, whilst tending to her mother in London, Caroline had asked over and over if Heather remembered anything about Lambkin. Her mother had tried desperately, furrowing her brow in concentration, scrunching her face as she sought any memory at all, but she could not even say what colour Lambkin's eyes were.

"That's the grammar school there," Luke interjected from the driver's bench to the three women in the back. "Or what will be the grammar school. The house can't be far."

As much as Caroline loved him, it was possibly the worst thing he could have said.

"Perhaps, we should not intrude," Heather said abruptly, her face ashen. "Maybe, it would be better if I didn't visit with you. I haven't been any sort of mother to her. She will not know me, any more than I know her. Yes, I think I should stay with Luke in the cart, so as not to cause any trouble."

Esther flashed her mother a hard look. "You've come this far, Mother. You can go the rest of the way. You owe it to Lambkin." She hesitated. "Indeed, if you don't proceed, then I won't even consider forgiving you for all you have done. And I was almost at such a point, too."

It was unkind of Esther to use what Heather desired the most as a means of manipulation, but Caroline was not going to argue with her sister's methods. She, too, would have been furious if Heather had retreated at the last moment.

"You're right," Heather murmured. "I do owe it to her. I apologise."

"Thank you," Esther replied, a touch haughtily, as the expanse of Woodhouse Moor stretched away to the right and beautiful, red brick houses appeared on the left.

The moor was an expanse of open greenery, surrounded

by full-boughed, leafy trees that rustled in the faint breeze that offered no respite. Upon it, exquisite sandstone formed the beginnings of what would one day be the new grammar school, standing in considerable contrast to the almost orange tone of the red brick houses.

"There's only one opposite," Luke pointed out, bringing the cart to a standstill.

Sure enough, at the black iron gates of the first house, two stags stood guard. A lawned front garden bridged the gap between the gates and the porch, with room for a carriage to come in and out. A grand house, in truth—much grander than Caroline had expected. Three storeys high, with sash windows, a tall brick chimney, and, off to the right, what appeared to be a coach house.

"Isn't this the servants' entrance?" Esther asked, eyeing the residence.

Caroline frowned. "It seems to be, but I suppose she chose the description that would be easiest to locate."

"Either that, or the Hyles' don't want us coming in through the front door," Esther remarked, and though Caroline did not want to admit it, she wondered if her sister had a point.

Too eager to see Lambkin again to bother with the semantics of which entrance they could use, Caroline leaned forward to kiss Luke's cheek and got down from the cart.

"Don't go kidnapping anyone, do you hear?" he said with a smile.

"I'll try not to," Caroline replied, helping her mother and sister down to the pavement.

Locking her arm through Heather's, Caroline proceeded on through the gates and across the gravel drive between the lawns to what was almost certainly the servants' entrance. The porch was not elaborate, the steps not as steep, and there was a narrow window to the right of the door, for the housekeeper or butler to peer out and decide if whoever was knocking warranted permission to enter.

Let us hope we meet the requirements...

Caroline knocked before anyone could lose their nerve, for though she was determined to maintain an air of calm confidence, she had no real idea what to expect. Of course, she hoped that Mr. and Mrs. Hyles were everything they had promised to be, and that they had been genuine with their invitation, but she could not quite suppress *all* of her anxiety.

"She would be so lucky to be raised here," Heather whispered, clearly speaking her thoughts aloud as she glanced up the stretch of lawn to where pretty, walled gardens began, just visible through a small gate.

"She would be lucky to be raised with us," Esther retorted sharply. "*Now,* I mean. She won't want for anything, with all the money you'll receive from Papa's work."

Heather nodded hesitantly. "Yes, I suppose you're right."

Just then, the door opened, revealing a bespectacled woman of around forty or so, with a friendly face, and dark hair fashioned into a neat chignon.

"May I help you?" she asked amiably enough.

Caroline cleared her dry throat. "I am Caroline, this is my sister, Esther, and this is my mother, Heather Calder."

"And... what might I assist you with?" The woman frowned, showing no recognition whatsoever.

"We are Lambkin's family," Caroline answered. "The little girl who came to live here perhaps six weeks ago?"

"Mr. and Mrs. Hyles' adopted daughter," Esther added.

"She likely doesn't go by the name 'Lambkin' here, I expect."

Of course not. Caroline could have smacked herself. Still, she had expected the staff to at least know where Lambkin had come from—about her sisters, if nothing else.

The housekeeper's frown deepened, as if she were trying to remember where she had left her chatelaine. "Forgive me, ladies, but this is the residence of Mr. Farnham and his family."

"Oh…" Caroline's cheeks flamed with embarrassment, after all of her protesting that she had not mistaken the address. "Is there another house nearby with stags at the gate?"

The housekeeper shook her head. "Not that I know of, and I've been here many years. Nor, if I may, do I know of a Mr. and Mrs. Hyles."

Panic struck Caroline squarely in the chest, as she hurried to describe the couple: "Mr. Hyles is perhaps thirty, very handsome, with light brown hair and… I think his eyes were brown, too. Mrs. Hyles is younger, maybe twenty, and exceptionally beautiful. She has the most perfect teeth, blue eyes, and golden hair."

"Are you sure it was not *Hay*les?" the housekeeper asked, her expression grim.

"I… don't know." Caroline hesitated, wondering if she had heard wrong. "Possibly. Would you know of a Mr. and Mrs. Hayles?"

The woman nodded, her nose crinkling in distaste. "He was the butler here, until he was cast out for indecent behaviour with the scullery maid—a Miss Malston. Exceptionally beautiful, just as you described. A shame her character did not match." She pointed down the street. "His wife is the governess two houses down. Distraught, she was, poor thing."

"But that can't be," Caroline said, her head swimming. "They were husband and wife. They said they lived here. They were dressed well, they—"

"Stole many things before they ran off together," the housekeeper interrupted. "The constables have been searching for them since they left this house, so if you do find them, be sure to take them directly to the authorities. Indeed, I am sorry, but it would appear they have stolen more from you than they have from us, if your sister is with them."

With an apologetic smile, the housekeeper closed the door to the servants' entrance on them, leaving the three women standing there in a mutual daze. It was absurd. Impossible.

I must be mistaken about the house, and that woman must be mistaken about there being no Hyles' living nearby. But as much as Caroline tried to convince herself, she still found her legs moving almost involuntarily towards the house that the woman had pointed out.

She knocked on the servants' entrance door with such vigour that her knuckles throbbed, her heart in her throat as a man came to the door.

"Yes?" he asked more curtly than the housekeeper. "How can I help you?"

"Is there a Mrs. Hayles here?" Caroline replied, equally brusque.

The man frowned. "Please state your business."

"I have to speak to her with some urgency," Caroline replied, softening her tone. "It pertains to her husband. We were sent here by Mr. Farnham's housekeeper."

Let me be wrong. Let it be a mistake. Please...

The man's demeanour shifted slightly. "Very well. Wait here; I'll fetch her for you, though she won't thank you for troubling her in the midst of her day."

He closed the door and disappeared inside, once again leaving the three women to their thoughts, which grew more worrisome by the second.

"It has to be a mistake," Esther whispered, blanching of all colour. "We should knock on every house near here until we find them. It couldn't be the butler and the scullery maid. They were so... well-to-do. Even with stolen clothes, they wouldn't be able to... *pretend* to be of higher society than they are."

Caroline clawed an anxious hand through her hair. "Who better to mimic the upper classes than the servants?"

"Don't say that!" Esther yelped, her eyes wide. "Please, don't say that. I'll never forgive myself."

In that moment, Caroline understood the horror she saw in her sister's eyes. Although Caroline was the one who had eventually agreed to let Lambkin go, she was also the one who had stubbornly tried to fight to keep her at Fox House. *Esther* was the one who had encouraged the adoption; without her words about selfishness and how wonderful Lambkin's life would be with the Hyles', there was no way that Caroline would have relinquished their youngest sister into the care of that couple.

"Is she lost to us?" Heather asked meekly.

"No," Esther barked. "No, she isn't. She can't be. This is all a misunderstanding; I am certain of it."

As certain as you were that the Hyles' were a lovely couple who would do well by Lambkin? Caroline held the retort back, for it would do no good to snipe amongst themselves.

A short while later, Caroline's nerves dancing on a knife edge, the door opened again. A relatively young woman, similar in age to Mr. Hyles, peered out with a suspicious gaze.

"I was told you wanted to speak to me," she said tightly. "About my husband?"

Caroline did not hesitate, jumping into the story of how she and her sisters had come to meet Mr. Fox, and how that wretched man had located a couple who had shown an interest in adopting Lambkin. She described the couple, watching the woman's face as it grew more and more irate.

"They seemed to be known to him in some capacity," she said desperately. "They were not complete strangers to him."

Which should have been a warning to begin with…

Mrs. Hayles sniffed. "Then, I suggest you speak with this Mr. Fox."

"I can't," Caroline gasped, her lungs threatening to explode. "He was hanged yesterday."

The woman stared, her mouth falling open. "You mean… *that* Mr. Fox? The one from the papers? The… child killer?"

Caroline nodded, words failing her.

"Well, I… am sorry for all you have clearly suffered," Mrs. Hayles said, her tone a note less harsh, "but I still can't help you find your sister. All I can tell you is that my husband is *not* married to that… despicable girl. He is still married to me, unfortunately. And though I know they remained in Leeds for a while, the last time they were seen was a month ago. With constables searching for them, I do not imagine they are here anymore, or anywhere near here. I'm sorry."

The scorned woman moved to close the door, but Caroline's hand shot out, holding it open.

"Why would they 'adopt' a child? Do you know

anything about a child?" she wheezed, her eyes blurry. "Please, Mrs. Hayles. Please... this is my sister."

Mrs. Hayles hesitated. "I know nothing about a child, Miss." She furrowed her brow. "All I know is that my husband was so desperate for a son or daughter that he abandoned me for that scullery maid, when it was discovered that I could not bear children. If he has done this, which it seems he has, I suspect he wanted the young, beautiful 'bride' *and* a child, whether she could bear his children or not."

"She said she couldn't," Caroline choked, her legs shaking violently.

"Then, there is your answer. Now, if you will excuse me." Mrs. Hayles offered a fleeting look of apology, and closed the door in Caroline's face.

For several minutes, Caroline stayed there, her hand pressed to the door, leaning forwards until her legs decided to cooperate. She could not even begin to think about looking back, certain that her own shock and horror would be reflected on the faces of her sister and mother.

"We have to find her," Esther croaked, as if that course of action were not obvious. "She is out there somewhere with charlatans and liars! They have stolen her, Caro!"

"And it is all my fault..." The unspoken part echoed just as loudly, though Caroline would not be the one to lay blame upon Esther's door. Esther would punish herself enough as it was.

Caroline swallowed thickly. "Of course, we must do everything within our power to get her back."

"I will hunt them down if it is the last thing that I do," Heather said suddenly, her voice brimming with more strength than Caroline had ever heard from her mother before.

And as she turned, Caroline saw that same strength, etched upon her mother's face, burning in her eyes, making her look, for just a moment, like the mother they had known before Quentin had destroyed their lives. A woman who would have done anything to protect her children.

But where do we start? Caroline held her tongue, wishing she had the same fire in her belly as her mother. For although she, too, wanted to move heaven and Earth to retrieve Lambkin, how were they even supposed to *begin* searching for two talented liars who had seemingly vanished without a trace?

Indeed, if the constables could not find them, what chance did the Calders have?

ALSO BY NELL HARTE

The Ragged Mudlarke

The Little Lost One

The Pit Girl's Courage

The Midnight Watcher

The Blind Taylor's Daughter

The Little Orphan's Christmas Miracle

The Nurses Plight

The Orphaned Street Picker

The Wretched Wreath Seller

The Orphan Thieves

The Whitechapel Wife

The Slum Widow

The Stolen Street Girl

The Little Chimney Sweep Girl

The Abandoned Waif's Christmas Miracle

The Millworkers Daughter

The Midwife's Plight

The Slum Dweller

The Barrow Girl

The Slum Widow

THANK YOU FOR READING MY BOOKS

I hope that you enjoyed this book.

If you are willing to leave a short and honest review for me on Amazon, it will be very much appreciated, as reviews help to get my books noticed.

Join my Newsletter

Receive A Subscriber Only Book

CLICK HERE FOR

THE BEGGAR URCHINS

JOIN MY NEWSLETTER

Join my Newsletter
   Receive A Subscriber Only Book
   The Beggar Thieves

Printed in Dunstable, United Kingdom